I realized we'd miscalculated our negotiating posture when the Knessi ambassador leaned across the table and bit off Kari Sheldon's right hand. The senior member of the human delegation stared down at her mangled arm for several seconds with a puzzled expression, then swayed as shock overwhelmed her physical resources. She was already losing consciousness by the time we overcame our own momentary paralysis. Victor had a pressure pad around the stump within seconds and I found enough voice to request an adjournment.

From "Empirical Facts"

Managansett Press

Don D'Ammassa is the author of:

Horror
Blood Beast
Servant of Chaos*
Caverns of Chaos*
Wings over Manhattan
The Gargoyle
That Way Madness Lies*
Little Evils*
Passing Death*
Date with the Dark*
The Devil Is in the Details*
Living Things*
Shadows Over R'Lyeh*

Science Fiction
Scarab*
Haven*
Narcissus*
Translation Station
The Sinking Island*
Alien & Otherwise*
Wormdance*
Sandcastles*
Carbon Copies*
Phantom of the Space Opera*

Mysteries
Murder in Silverplate*
Dead of Winter*
Death at the Art Gallery*
Death on the Mountain*
Death on Black Island*
Death in Black and White*

Fantasy
The Kaleidoscope*
Elaborate Lies*
The Maltese Gargoyle*
Perilous Pursuits*
Multiplicity*
The Hippogriff of the Baskervilles*

Nonfiction
The Encyclopedia of Science Fiction
The Encyclopedia of Fantasy & Horror
The Encyclopedia of Adventure Fiction
Masters of Detection Vol I*
Masters of Detection Vol II*
Masters of Detection Vol III*
Architects of Tomorrow Vol I*

*published by Managansett Press

2

# ALIEN & OTHERWISE

"Empirical Facts" first appeared in *Absolute Magnitude*, 1996
"Realizations" first appeared in *Whitley Strieber's Aliens*, 1999
"Book Day" first appeared in *The Gloaming*, 2011
"The Karma Sutra" first appeared in *Analog*, 1999
"Shadow and Substance" first appeared in *Figment*, 1993
"Ahead of His Time" first appeared in *Space Trails*, 2010
"Martyrs" first appeared in *Panverse 3*, 2011
All other stories appear for the first time in this volume.

Managansett Press First Edition 2015

# ALIEN & OTHERWISE

# CONTENTS

# EMPIRICAL FACTS

I realized we'd miscalculated our negotiating posture when the Knessi ambassador leaned across the table and bit off Kari Sheldon's right hand. The senior member of the human delegation stared down at her mangled arm for several seconds with a puzzled expression, then swayed as shock overwhelmed her physical resources. She was already losing consciousness by the time we overcame our own momentary paralysis. Victor had a pressure pad around the stump within seconds and I found enough voice to request an adjournment.

"We wish to consider your objection to our proposal in some detail before responding." My voice was unsteady, but the Knessi had given no indication they were sensitive to human emotional states.

Ambassador Gnocki scratched at the distinctive scar that disfigured his chest while the Govanni interpreter translated Terran standard to whatever passed for language among the Knessi. They always used Govanni to communicate with "lesser" races, and our intelligence services insisted that information was being passed by means other than simple sounds. Too much data was communicated in very brief exchanges to admit of any other explanation. Limited telepathy was a common but unsubstantiated theory although no one had come up with a plausible scenario in which three meter tall, scale armored predators with horny beaks would have developed such an ability.

There were a lot of things we didn't understand about the Knessi, things we needed to learn in a hurry if the human race was going to survive, let alone prosper.

"Should we take her back to the ship or use the local facilities?" Janis Fong remained, as usual, calm and collected. Officially she was an observer, not a diplomat, but we all knew she represented the military. The high command still hadn't accepted the fact that their hundred or so warships amounted to little compared to an empire that reportedly controlled many thousands of star systems. According to Glakker, the Govanni liaison assigned to us, the several dozen dreadnoughts accompanying Ambassador Gnocki represented the usual escort for a minor ambassador.

"And these their most current ships are not, Human Alan Nkruma. Gnocki a scandal has committed. Many powerful enemies among his people has he made, and they to this remote and unimportant frontier region have him exiled." Our reconnaissance holos supported his claim that these were not state of the art warships. Several of them clearly were in sore need of drydocking and a refit.

I suddenly realized that I was in charge of the delegation, at least until Kari came around. "We'll use our own. The Knessi would probably interpret it as a sign of weakness if we asked for their help."

"We're not exactly negotiating from a position of strength anyway, Alan." Victor's voice was tinged with barely controlled panic.

"All the more reason not to relinquish whatever dignity remains to us."

The Knessi wouldn't rise until we'd departed. To do so would, as we understood their psychology, concede to us some degree of ownership of these chambers. Knessi, for all their technological superiority, were clearly still influenced by their more primitive natures. They were fiercely territorial, their lives were governed by elaborate and pervasive rituals, and they consumed most of their food by hunting it down, usually in special preserves they built on every world they occupied.

I hoped fervently that Kari's hand gave the ambassador indigestion.

Victor used his cyberwand to neutralize the security shield protecting our quarters and we carried Sheldon to the med unit. Once our head of mission was sedated and under treatment, I called a staff meeting to consider our options. Victor Knabbi seemed more agitated than ever, Janis Fong her usual imperturbable self, the remaining dozen members of the delegation scattered across the intervening spectrum.

"I think we should request a delay to consult with our superiors." Everett Carr was, in my opinion, ill suited for this assignment, had questioned every initiative we'd suggested since arriving in the Delta Pavonis system.

"It may come to that," I conceded, "but I'd like to hear some alternatives first."

"We could withdraw in protest," Janis suggested mildly. "It looks to me like Gnocki is trying to prove he's an alpha male and can't be dominated. Sometimes bullies fold when their bluff is called."

"That fleet out there is hardly a bluff," argued Victor.

"It's a formidable but not insurmountable obstacle," conceded Janis. "Our analysis indicates we could take them, though with significant losses. I'd prefer it not come to that, but we do have to recognize that our fleet provides a credible threat and we could have them in this system in a matter of days."

"They'd be able to handle the ambassador's entourage, perhaps, but it wouldn't take the Knessi long to bring additional forces from other systems. We don't have any idea of their true strength in this region." It was Everett again, more agitated than ever. "Don't forget what happened to the Passaqualia and the Denovans."

"We only have the Knessi's word for that."

"The Govanni, actually," I interrupted. "And if it's true, there aren't any Passaqualia or Denovans left to ask about it."

Glakker was fluent and communicative and had demonstrated an extraordinary willingness to discuss the past exploits of the race he served. "The Knessi no weakness or mercy have," he'd told us. "Once another great empire they encountered. The Llyriani many hundreds of planets controlled and a fleet of ships more powerful even than that of the Knessi was assembled. But the Knessi after many hundreds of planets died to cease fighting refused. The Llyriani to end the slaughter finally surrendered."

I'd felt a degree of admiration for the Knessi despite their menace when Glakker told us that story, but he'd chilled our blood with its sequel. "The Llyriani to disband their military agreed, and their entire species later executed was. The Knessi could not any future threat accept."

There was uncomfortable tension as we tried to decide on a course of action. I let the staff argue for a while until it was clear that we were split into two camps. Everett, Victor, and Alis Lee wanted to withdraw from negotiations and kick the problem upstairs. With the exception of Janis Fong and Sirash Ngui, the remainder wanted me to keep the discussion alive but stagnant until Kari was able to return to duty. Janis kept her own council after her initial comments, and I had the distinct impression she was holding something back. Sirash was an historian who was supposed to be recording our mission for posterity; he had no official standing but had always struck me as intelligent and perceptive, though reluctant to express an opinion.

"All right, I think we've done all we can for now. I'm going to confer with Glakker and see if he has anything constructive to offer. Gnocki won't agree to another session today anyway so let's think about our options and hope Kari's able to give us some guidance tomorrow." She would be physically capable of returning to duty within twenty-four hours, but if I'd been in her position, I'm not sure I'd have stepped into a room with Gnocki again. He might still be hungry.

Glakker was perfectly willing to discuss the situation with me, in my quarters or his. Curious, I suggested the latter.

Delta Pavonis is a fairly new Knessi acquisition. There are, according to Glakker and our own sketchy intelligence, less than a dozen of the master race on the fourth planet, along with two hundred Govanni and several thousand Miri, a small, quasi-mammalian species with limited intelligence but an apparently limitless capacity for work. The Miri provided all of the menial labor in the colony, but were regarded by even the Govanni as little more than bright animals. Glakker told me that once fully developed, the planet would be home to something on the order of a hundred Knessi and that the other populations would swell proportionately.

"The Knessi no more on a single world this size will allow. To each a certain amount of land must given be, and other sufficient to hold many thousands of servants must aside be held." The dependence on what amounted to little more than slave labor in such a highly developed culture was anomalous, but Glakker had told the ambassador and I that it was a matter of prestige rather than actual physical dependence. "The Knessi always their personal power must prove."

Govanni buildings were invariably single story. According to Glakker, this was because it would shame a Knessi to ever have to lift its eyes to see a member of a lesser species, but I thought it might just as easily derive from the Miri's racial fear of heights. According to Glakker, they originated on a featureless planet covered with grasslands and hadn't progressed much beyond wheels and levers at the time they were incorporated into the Knessi empire. The Govanni might be a subject species themselves, but they were clearly willing to exploit someone even lower in the pecking order.

I found Glakker's quarters easily from his directions, and was ushered by a Miri into a plainly furnished room that could have been home to a human being if one ignored the squatting chamber in the dining area and the fact that there was no way to close off the entranceway. The Govanni defecated openly and expressed amusement with our human preoccupation with privacy. The lack of a door was a product of what our intelligence interpreted as a racial claustrophobia.

"Greetings, Human Alan Nkruma."

"Greetings, Govanni Glakker Besarra Nakar."

"Today's session disagreeable was."

I nodded, then answered affirmatively. The Govanni were good at picking up non-verbal cues but sometimes they misunderstood their implications. "Have we somehow distressed the Knessi?"

Glakker clicked his tongues together but I had no idea whether it was an expression of sympathy, frustration, or possibly humor. "Even now, the Knessi we Govanni do not always understand."

"How long have your people worked for the Knessi?"

"Almost one hundred generations have we served." That made it about five thousand years. I shook my head in amazement.

"Belief in my statement you lack?" I could tell by the fibrillation of his dorsal crest that Glakker was agitated.

"No, not at all." Glakker had misinterpreted my gesture as a negative. "I was expressing my own difficulty assimilating this data."

"Serving the Knessi advantages provides. Govanni worlds by other races were sometimes attacked. Now the Knessi's protection has our shield been. We the first of their servants are."

"Of course." I wondered if I'd ever be able to tell whether or not Glakker was sincere in his loyalty to the Knessi. I wanted to believe that there was smoldering resentment here as well, that the rule of the Knessi was not as absolute as we'd been led to believe.

"Then the Govanni were the first race the Knessi encountered?"

"The Govanni the first allowed to survive were," was the disturbing answer. "Knessi because we could speak to them our presence tolerated. To stay in your own region of space and avoid contact better is."

"But we know there are unexplored systems in this region, thousands of them. Surely the Knessi will allow us to expand away from their sphere of influence."

"Knessi all other races suspect find. If continue to expand you insist, your destruction they eventually seek will."

I thought about that. "You're saying there's no room for negotiation at all here, only surrender. My people aren't likely to find that acceptable."

"Few other paths to consider exist."

I returned to our quarters a short time later, profoundly disturbed and acutely depressed.

Kari Sheldon was conscious and articulate the following morning, but she had no intention of returning to the negotiations immediately. "Let's see how the Ambassador reacts to being forced to deal with a subordinate for a while." She gave me an apologetic look. "Our best analysis is that this is something of a pissing contest, so maybe we can put Gnocki off his feed for a while." She grimaced as she realized what she'd just said, but pushed on.

"We need more information. Any word from your sources, Janis?"

"Very little. We've sent flitterships to some of the systems the Knessi claim, but we haven't found any of their military bases as yet."

This was news to me and I frowned. "The Govanni have warned us about provocative acts. If the Knessi find out we've been spying on them..."

"We'll be no worse off than we are already." Janis let her calm exterior ruffle a bit for the first time in my experience. "There's still a chance this is all just a shell game."

"I'm not following this." I wasn't.

Kari uneasily shifted her wounded hand. "Alan, we have reason to believe that the Knessi forces in this area of space aren't as numerous as we've been led to believe."

"You mean the Govanni have been lying to us?"

"Not necessarily. But they're an enslaved people, have been for centuries. The Knessi clearly don't consider them allies and aren't likely to have told them everything."

"All right, it's a dangerous game, but I suppose it's worth playing. So what do we do next?"

"We stall for a while, see what happens. I've already called off today's session, and you'll be sitting in for me tomorrow, Alan."

I was, I admit it, miffed. As second in command of the mission, I should have known what our policy was beforehand. Obviously Janis Fong's role was more than just advisory, in fact, I began to wonder if she might not actually be Sheldon's superior. It would explain her occasional deference to the "advisor" during staff meetings. Childishly, I sulked in my quarters for the rest of the brief day, waiting until darkness fell across the Govanni "city", which in human terms wasn't much more than a small town.

Then I sneaked out.

We weren't supposed to leave the government complex without a Govanni guide, theoretically for our own protection, particularly at night. "Knessi in darkness sometimes hunt. For this purpose the forest south of our city aside is set, but sometimes the rule disregarded is. No one but Knessi forbid each other can."

Pedestrian traffic had almost entirely ceased. The Govanni had very poor night vision, and since much of their language was conducted by visual cues, they found it difficult to function in the darkness. Miri slept almost catatonically when darkness fell, and I saw them curled up into balls everywhere I looked. The night's silence was palpable.

I didn't have a specific goal in mind; I was just determined to commit a small, personal rebellion. To this day I'm not certain whether I was acting against the tyranny of the Knessi or the wishes of my superiors, neither of whom had been entirely forthright of late.

I headed north, away from the hunting preserve, toward the Knessi compound.

Although we'd scanned the area from space, we'd come planetside in a Govanni piloted shuttle. Human spacecraft were restricted to an orbit well distant from the planet's hidden defense systems. Ambassador Gnocki was ensconced in the largest of three Knessi enclaves, each surrounded by meter thick walls of a ceramic material, small fortresses with only a single entrance.

"The Knessi creatures of tradition are," explained Govanni. "only in the pattern of their early civilization do they build."

If true I presumed the Knessi home world must have been,

might still be, a place of constant violence. The entrance was narrow, guarded by Govanni during the daylight, shielded by an energy shell in the darkness. Absently I pointed my cyberwand in its direction and cycled through a range of frequencies, not really expecting anything to happen.

The shell flickered and dissipated.

For a moment, I wanted to turn and run like hell, run all the way back to my quarters and hide under the bed. But curiosity is a powerful human trait, and I was feeling sorry for myself because I'd been left out of the information loop by my superiors, and finally I said what the hell and went inside.

There was a single, blocklike building within the compound, its material of construction the same as that of the outer walls. There were no windows, and once again a single entrance which, like Govanni structures, seemed to have no door.

I crossed the open space and entered there as well. It was much bigger on the inside than on the outside, because the interior was cut into the ground, a recessed chamber surrounded by a balcony on all sides. Ambassador Knessi stood below me, his ragged scar unmistakable, and he wasn't happy.

He was in fact chained to one wall while a half dozen Govanni stood a few meters away, gesticulating and speaking rapidly and simultaneously in their own language. They didn't appear to be particularly pleased either, and I had a feeling they'd be even less so if they discovered me spying on them.

Because in that split second, I understood what had been bothering me about the entire Knessi-Govanni setup.

It didn't make sense.

Don't get me wrong. I know that when there's a confrontation between individuals, might often prevails over reason, muscle over intellect, the claw over the brain. Sometimes, for short periods, the same holds true in the relations between nations and, presumably, between sentient races. But the Knessi just weren't bright enough to maintain an interstellar empire for scores of generations, no matter how superior they were as warriors. They weren't smart enough to create sophisticated weaponry. Possibly they confiscated some from their subject peoples, but a race so bound by tradition would be unlikely to adapt readily to an entirely new style of warfare.

The Knessi weren't the master race; it was the Govanni who

were calling the shots.

I sneaked out of the Knessi compound without being discovered and returned to the Terran compound.

Sheldon was officially outraged and unofficially offended that I'd disobeyed orders and "endangered the entire mission". Janis Fong was noncommittal, but treated me with considerably more respect afterwards. While she never actually admitted it, I think she admired my audacity, even if she suspected that it resulted from pique rather than courage.

She sent a coded message to our command ship that same evening.

Given this new perspective, the military's flittership changed the focus of their intelligence gathering missions and stepped up their clandestine operation while we allowed the Govanni to drag out negotiations on Delta Pavonis. Delay worked in our favor. I spent as much time as possible with Glakker, who seemed convinced that I was swallowing his story without reservation.

The Govanni were clearly disconcerted when out fleet arrived in force a month later, and we in turn were surprised when the purportedly seasoned Knessi fleet surrendered almost without firing a shot. We'd learned that the empire had a hollow center, but hadn't expected to discover that most of the bristling weapon bays were mockups, or that those guns which were functional had almost no ammunition.

Two years passed before I ran into Janis Fong again.

My career had progressed well despite what my superiors called "a distressing lack of respect for his superiors". The Knessi "empire" was revealed as less than two hundred worlds, each of which hastily surrendered to the first human ship to appear in its skies. The Knessi themselves turned out to be only marginally sapient, clever domesticated animals the Govanni had transformed into the bogeyman to overawe less than two dozen other species, most of which welcomed human intervention with open arms, or other appropriate appendages. The Llyriani, Passaqualia, and Denovans turned out to be entirely fictional.

I was vacationing on Wunderbar when I ran into Janis Fong quite by accident. She invited me out for a stim, one thing led to another, eventually to some clumsy but ultimately satisfying sex in her suite.

"Tell me something, Janis," I said quietly after we'd recovered from our exertions. "It was really you in charge back there on Delta Pavonis, wasn't it? Sheldon was just a figurehead."

At first I didn't think she was going to answer, then she laughed and threw her head back against the pillow. "Actually, we had equal authority. Sirash was calling the shots."

"Sirash? The historian?"

"That's right. We already knew there was something fishy in the Knessi-Govanni setup. Too many inconsistencies. Too few hard facts. For one thing, if the Knessi were as all powerful as we'd been led to believe, it would have been much easier to find their installations. So it was decided that we should wrap ourselves in layers of deception as well."

"So my great discovery really wasn't all that important after all?"

She hesitated, then shrugged her shoulders. "It helped, but we were pretty close to reaching that conclusion from external evidence anyway. Fortunately we took the right action despite our mistake."

"Mistake?"

Her face tightened, then relaxed. "What the hell, it'll be made public soon anyway. Will you promise not to repeat this until it does?"

"I've taken the oath of confidentiality." I was still in the diplomatic corps, to the dismay of my superiors.

"The Govanni weren't really in charge either."

"But the Knessi are barely sapient."

"About chimpanzee level, that's right."

"Then who..."

"The Miri. They're a lot brighter than we thought."

"But I've been on their home planet. They don't even have a technological culture. Almost every artifact I saw there was brought from offworld."

Janis nodded. "Their planet has almost no accessible metals. They were largely nomadic until the Govanni landed and enslaved them. When their aptitude for technology became obvious, the Govanni saw a way to free themselves from performing most of the actual work in their society. They're real snobs about that, you know; that's why they stressed that the Knessi wanted to enslave their neighbors. They thought all species would feel the same way."

"Anyway, they enforced a breeding program and slowly replaced their own people in increasingly skilled professions. We're not sure exactly how long it took for the balance of power to shift. The Govanni themselves didn't realize they were no longer masters of their own society. Some don't admit it even now."

That was nearly thirty years ago. The Terran Empire stretches across eight hundred star systems and includes thirty-nine intelligent races now. Earth itself is the bustling capital of an expansive, thriving, multi-racial culture, and we humans are clearly proud of the society we've created.

But now that I'm retired, independently wealthy, and have the leisure to write the memoirs I've planned for most of my adult lifetime, those early years seem even more significant. I recall the computer error that prevented us from launching an ill-conceived economic assault on the Triashi Federation, the crash landing of the *Potemkin* that killed the leaders of the Revanchist Party and averted a disastrous internal conflict, and the revelation that Morgan Tetsui was secretly manipulating currency exchanges to repress the economies of certain worlds. A Miri programmed the computer, another piloted the *Potemkin*, and Tetsui employed an almost entirely Miri staff because they were so "reliable".

And I wonder whose empire this really is.

# PERFECT PITCH

I knew something was screwy when the Boston pitching staff opened the season with three perfect games. Sure, Blackwell is a topnotch hurler; he had three one hitters last year alone. I could even stretch my imagination to believe Garcia might manage a single brilliant game. But Norwood was strictly a finisher, and it was no secret that his arm was still sore from off season surgery. During his last three innings, as batters inexplicably missed one easy ball after another, the bleachers were strangely silent, as though no one could actually believe what they were seeing. The reporter sitting next to me in the press box looked as though he was experiencing physical pain.

I was with the crowd that caught Norwood coming out of the showers and he looked as stunned as everyone else. His smile kept slipping off to one side, as though it felt uncomfortable on his face.

"Everything just seemed to go right," he told us, but without conviction, inflecting the words so that they sounded more like a question than an explanation.

As senior sports editor for the *Journal*, I rarely travel with the team, but no one raised an eyebrow when I pulled rank and announced that I'd be flying out for the Detroit game. Vitarelli was pitching for the Sox, a steady man, but past his prime. He was on the last year of his current contract and no one expected it to be renewed. His fastball was slower every year, his curve straighter, and his slider rarely slid.

Vitarelli pitched a one hitter under the lights, and Boswell reached first base on an error. Another shutout.

Rather than allaying my suspicions, the trip added to them. I interviewed Vitarelli in the locker room after the game. We knew each other pretty well, having shared our rookie year, him pitching, me covering the games for the network. A few other stringers were hanging around and he answered their questions dutifully, but with uncharacteristically terse phrases. I waited until no one else was paying any attention.

"Is something wrong, Don?"

He glanced around, then nodded me over to an empty corner. Every locker room has its own distinctive odor, and this one was particularly rank. But it felt familiar, almost homey.

"I haven't seen you throw like that in a while, Don."

"Neither have I." He wasn't smiling, and shifted weight nervously from one foot to the other on the damp floor. "I don't understand it, Ted. The ball almost seemed alive. I swear sometimes it picked up speed after it left my hand."

During the flight back, I called the office and asked them to make a copy of that day's game tape and leave it in my office.

I watched it late that night, normal speed, slow motion, frame by frame, until my eyes were so leaden that I no longer trusted what I thought I was seeing. The city had grown as quiet as it ever does and I walked to my apartment window, stretching, wondering if it was all happenstance, a freak of air pressure, wind, and other factors, or if I was onto something big.

The mid-morning sun was so bright and cheerful that I almost dismissed my suspicions, but I brought the tape to an old friend at MIT anyway.

Dr. Norma Chen specializes in ballistics, and has worked for the federal government as well as consulting for local law enforcement agencies. We had graduated from high school together, even dated a few times, and still met for lunch once or twice a year. I explained my problem and handed her the tape, then followed her through a maze of corridors to a small projection room.

She played the portion of the tape that I was interested in at normal speed, nodded to herself, then again in slow motion.

"Most unusual," she said at last. "And quite impossible. I don't need to do a simulation for this one. The changes of speed and direction..." she spread her arms wide and let them drop. "There has to be an outside force involved."

"But what outside force?"

Dr. Chen had no answer for that. The next day, I watched the Sox give up a total of three hits in a double header with the Braves, and two days later Blackwell pitched his second perfect game of the year.

I borrowed tapes of each game and found the same anomaly. Time after time, at the last possible moment, the ball quite literally jumped away from the swinging bat. On those rare occasions when an opposition player actually hit the ball, it was almost always fielded easily, in one case after literally hanging motionless in the sky for a full second, giving outfielder Jensen time to run under it and make the play. The rare successful hit seemed artificial, a clumsy and inadequate attempt to disguise what was happening.

Some of my fellow reporters were also beginning to smell a rat and I knew I would have to move fast if the story was going to be an exclusive.Hacking into the league's main database, I cross referenced attendance lists and came up with over two hundred people who had yet to miss a Red Sox game. This didn't include walk-ins, corporate guests, and general admissions, but I suspected my quarry was a season ticket holder able to travel around the country for road games. One of the other players might have been responsible, but I doubted it; a professional would have been more careful, interfering only when absolutely necessary. Two games later, I had winnowed the list down to 195, still too many to be manageable.

Then Boston nearly lost its first game of the season, at home, winning four to two in the ninth inning. Three of the names remaining on my list had missed the game.

The first, Elroy Carpenter, had the best excuse. He'd died of consumptive heart failure the night before. His widow was the second, and when I called and identified myself, she asked whether I'd be willing to buy two season tickets for which she had no further use.

The third name was Corinne Conway.

Corinne hesitated briefly before agreeing to see me. I had called and told her I was doing a feature on the reaction of Red Sox season ticket holders to their amazing opening run and had chosen her name as part of a random sample. We met in a small restaurant in Cambridge, took a sidewalk table, and sipped white wine in the bright sunlight while waiting for our food to arrive.

"So how did you get interested in baseball, Ms Conway?"

She was in her late twenties, I guessed, mildly pretty, or she would have been had she deigned to smile.

"My father and brothers first, then my husband. Ex-husband, actually."

"Second generation Red Sox fan?"

"Actually, Dad liked the Yankees. Bill, my ex, was for the Sox, but he just liked the game in general. Didn't matter who was playing. He'd walk over to the park and watch the kids all summer long."

She hadn't smiled once since we'd met, but she didn't seem to be at all uneasy. I couldn't be positive that Corinne was the person I was looking for, but I had a gut feeling that I was on the right track.

"So you come by your interest honestly," I quipped. "It's been a long time since the Sox have had such a great start."

"I suppose so."

"I guess you'd do just about anything to help them win this year," I prodded.

She'd been letting her attention wander around the room, but now she turned her head and met my eyes squarely. There was a brief, humorless smile, and she nodded. "You might say that." And I knew I was right.

"The pitching has been almost perfect, at least up until the game with the Indians. They didn't act like the team they'd been just two days earlier. I guess they needed your support."

"I missed my flight," she explained. "An accident on the way to the airport."

"You must be really devoted if you're willing to follow the team all around the country."

There was an unusually long pause before she answered, during which her face approximated but never quite achieved a readable expression. Suddenly she visibly relaxed, and let herself smile warmly. "Actually, I loathe baseball." She paused to let that register. "My mother died when I was very young, Mr. Welles. It was bad enough taking care of my father and three brothers during the off season; once spring came, I was weekend ballpark attendant in my own home. And then I met Bill, and foolishly married him, determined to get out of that house, and found myself chained to a man who'd rather watch baseball than have sex."

Her face was a study in aloof amusement, and I realized she knew that I knew, although I didn't know what exactly it was that I knew. After several long, silent seconds, she asked me a question.

"What do you suppose would happen if the Sox had a perfect season? Never lost a game, I mean."

I thought about it for a moment. "There'd be the biggest audience of all time toward the end, and then a letdown because the record would be unbreakable."

"And what if afterward it turned out that they had had outside help? That in effect, they had cheated."

The implications were unfolding rapidly in my mind, but before I could respond, she twisted the blade. "And what if it was shown that there was no way to prevent such manipulation if it happened again?"

A slow dawning of realization. "It would destroy the game. The results would have nothing to do with the quality of the teams."

"Exactly." And now she was smiling quite openly, but not pleasantly. I was still trying to find words when the waiter brought our check, set it down beside my coffee cup and walked away.

Just as I started to reach for it, Corinne turned her head, stared intently, and the slip of paper jumped into the air and flew directly to her hand.

"This one's on me," she said quietly.

# REALIZATIONS

When her father admitted he was color blind, Connie immediately wanted to see the what the world looked like through his eyes.

"You mean reds and greens are all backward?" She was ten years old.

"Not exactly. They're just not the same and sometimes I can't tell one shade from another."

"Then what colors DO you see?"

She hadn't understood that their frames of reference could be so different that the question was meaningless.

Almost twenty years later, she faced the same problem on an even greater scale.

"Are you all right, Dr. Jensen?"

Connie raised her head and pushed back from the console. "Yes, just tired."

"Can I get you some coffee?"

"That would be fine, Margery." She wouldn't drink it, just wanted to dismiss the technician without offending her.

The last message from Rikashi was still on the screen, just as impenetrable as ever.

"You are unusually purple today, Connie Jensen. You should kill someone softly."

"Lovely sentiment." A male voice spoke from the back of the room.

Connie blinked, disoriented, glanced over her shoulder. Colin Kraft had entered the interview room with his usual unconscious stealth.

"You're anthromorphizing again, Colin." Kraft was ostensibly a White House liaison, but everyone knew he worked for the NSC. Rikashi had only mentioned him once in his messages, an offhand reference to "the oblique one with the scoured mind". It made more sense than most of the alien's communications, which probably meant they understood even less than they thought they did.

"Colin is here if you wish to speak to him," she typed.

A new row of characters etched themselves onto the screen.

"Duality endures. Opportunity for fulfillment offers itself. Do you grasp?"

Kraft eased into the adjacent chair without an invitation. He had from time to time made casual sexual advances to Connie, but she had sensed his underlying disinterest. In a moment of insight, she'd realized he was sexless, adopting the pose as part of his mask.

"Still looks pretty random to me. Maybe our first alien visitor is insane. Maybe that's why so much of what it says is meaningless." He glanced at the upper monitor, a segmented screen showing the alien's living quarters from four separate views. Rikashi stood at the computer terminal, his vaguely human shaped body covered with millions of tiny cilia that moved as though they had individual life. Every few days he shed about five percent of them. New growth reached maturity within a week.

"Not at all. He just recognized your arrival and suggested that I murder you to reduce my purpleness. And we've established that Rikashi is male, Colin, not an 'it'." More or less, anyway. The exchange was just playacting. Connie had no doubt at all that Kraft had personal access to every progress report she and the rest of the staff turned in, and probably their private notes as well.

"Charming fellow. Wish we knew how it sensed our comings and goings. Do you suppose it's telepathic?"

"There's no evidence supporting that hypothesis."

Dr. Schroeder had asked that very question, and Rikashi had replied, "Darkness illuminates." Maybe he could see through the walls.

"Anything new from the recovery team?"

"How would I know? According to CNN they haven't found anything but insignificant fragments scattered across the ocean floor."

"Your mind is pink but your lips are blue." It slipped out before she realized it.

Kraft frowned. "Is that supposed to mean something."

"No, just thinking aloud." She turned back to the screen, satisfied that she'd called the man a liar as Rikashi might have done, and even more satisfied to know he'd read her interpretation of that phrase in her last report.

He said nothing when he left a moment later and Connie didn't watch him go.

"Release flees sideways to your future. I taste salt and sour and the air moves fitfully."

Connie checked the telltales quickly, fearing something had gone amiss with the environmental controls, but they hadn't varied. Rikashi could survive Earth's atmosphere but he was more comfortable with a lower proportion of oxygen and a different mix of trace elements. Could he be referring to her own breathing?

"Understanding remains elusive. We value life and will not take another for small reason."

"You must realize life's changes never end. To restore balance is a grand endeavor. We are red together in our sweet bones and flesh, Connie Jensen. Your time is always within my mind."

Connie chose to interpret that as a compliment. She needed one desperately.

"This situation is unacceptable!" Paul Mitchelson was theoretically the head of the contact team, although everyone knew that Kraft - presently sitting quietly in a corner - was pulling, or more frequently jerking the strings. "The creature is obviously intelligent, speaks English fluently, never sleeps, and is always willing to communicate. You've had four months to study it, and the only facts we're certain of could be summarized on a single page."

Connie felt no impulse to defend herself, but Julian Ngambo was clearly upset and spoke without being recognized.

"You underestimate the difficulties, Mr. Director. This isn't some isolated human tribe we're dealing with here. Rikashi comes from a totally different culture, a different biology and psychology. We're not even sure that language serves the same function with his people that it does with humans. There have been indications that these beings may possess some temporal sensory abilities..."

Mitchelson cut him off impatiently. "If the creature could travel in time, why doesn't it hop back to its ship and prevent it from crashing in the first place?"

Connie sighed. No one had implied Rikashi could travel in time physically, but there was some evidence that the alien occasionally responded to events that had not yet taken place, or which had happened weeks earlier. Unofficially they were calling it the Vonnegut Effect.

The meeting ended with increasingly strident exhortations to achieve a breakthrough. "In case it escaped your attention, at least four more escape pods entered the Earth's atmosphere, and three of them came down in China. I don't have to tell you what could happen if the Communists steal a march on us, do I?"

Someone was slumped in the corridor, leaning against the door to her apartment. Connie hesitated. The nights were growing colder in Virginia and while Maclean didn't have a large homeless population, they were around if you looked for them. She couldn't resent anyone wanting to come inside where it was warm, but she also needed to get into her apartment, and her bed, before she dropped from exhaustion.

"Excuse me, please?" She tried to sound both friendly and firm as she extended the key toward the door. The figure beneath her stirred, raised its head.

"Sarah? What are you doing here?"

"Came to visit," her eighteen year old sister answered sullenly. "I had to get out of that place."

Connie bit back the first words that came to mind, unlocked the door and led the way inside.

"Does Uncle Bob know where you are?"

Sarah rolled her eyes. "I'm fine, sis, thanks for asking. No, he doesn't know. If I'd left him a note, he'd've been here waiting for me."

"I'm going to call him right now." She started to fish around in her purse for her address book, but Sarah snatched it away.

"Wait...one...minute!" The younger girl was clearly furious. "At least give me a chance to tell you my side of the story first."

I really don't need this, Connie told herself, not right now. "All right, let's sit and talk."

"I can't live there any more, Connie. I just can't. I'm not going back. They don't want me there anyway."

"Don't talk nonsense. Uncle Bill volunteered to take us in when Mom and Dad died, you know. No one made him do it."

"I realize that." Sarah bit her lip, averted her eyes. "But ever since...you know...it hasn't been the same. I don't think he ever forgave me for running off and...and everything. And since he and Mary got married last year, well, it's just like I don't belong there any more."

"But that's your home now, Sarah. Where else can you go?"

Sarah faced her again, eyes brittle with tears. "I thought maybe I could stay with you for awhile. Sleep on your couch, clean house for you." She gestured vaguely at the chaos of the apartment, dirty dishes on the counters, newspapers tossed into corners, dirty laundry populating small colonies around the furniture. "Not that you need it or anything." A ghost of a smile, quickly gone. "And I could look around for a job. I'm eighteen, Connie. It's time for me to start living again."

"What about Doctor Martin? She's been very good for you."

"Yeah, I guess so. But she says I have to start doing the healing myself, that I'm using her to avoid dealing with my future. I think she's right."

They talked some more and eventually Connie called their uncle and told him Sarah would be staying with her for a few weeks. She thought he was more relieved to hear that than he had been to discover his niece was safe.

Rikashi never slept so the interview rooms were staffed around the clock. Connie swapped with Dr. Kelso for the graveyard shift for a few days because she suspected that the alien's behavior fluctuated diurnally even though the habitat was isolated from the outside world.

That's how she happened to be on duty when the alarms went off.

They had just completed another puzzling exchange in which she'd tried to learn the reason his people had come to Earth's system. Rikashi kept repeating that "the purpose of life is change" and "the purpose of change is life", and insisted that Connie's purple was growing deeper. She was reviewing the transcript when lights began flashing and a buzzer sounded.

Instinctively she glanced at the monitor, saw Rikashi unfold his two meter tall body from where it crouched(?) in one corner.

A mature tabby cat stepped out from between the alien's legs and began to clean itself.

Dr. Irving burst into the room, pointing at the screen. "Do you see that, Connie? Where the hell did that come from? The security people are going to shit bricks!"

Connie watched, fascinated, as Rikashi approached the cat. The animal showed no sign of alarm, not even when those writhing, cilia covered arms wrapped around its body.

"Do you suppose he's going to eat it?"

"Why would he? We supply all the food he wants, and with the right chemical structure."

"Maybe he wants dessert."

The cat was almost invisible now, completely enfolded by the cilia but showing no sign of panic. Rikashi bent his body forward slowly, obscuring the animal completely, then straightened up.

The cat was gone, as if it had never been there in the first place.

"First of all," Mitchelson said quietly, "it was not an hallucination. Hallucinations don't show up on film." The oversized screen flashed, then replayed the cat's brief visit to the isolation chamber. "Security has gone over the facility in great detail and we are satisfied that the integrity of the containment area was not breached by any conventional means." He paused a moment to let that sink in.

"If there was any doubt at all in your minds about the urgency of solving this problem before our friends in China do, or even our supposed German friends for that matter, I trust this will erase it."

Margery inclined her head toward Connie and whispered clandestinely. "I guess we can take that as confirmation of the rumor that the Germans recovered the missing pod."

But Connie wasn't paying attention. She was thinking about the brief exchange she'd had before security pulled everyone out of the complex for debriefing.

"Where did the cat come from, Rikashi?" She'd typed the words with trembling fingers, backspacing twice to correct mistakes.

"Life's potential is in all places. Life's purpose is life's purpose."

The session lasted through the morning and into the afternoon. By the time they called it quits for the day, Connie was afraid she'd nod off on the drive home.

Sarah kept the apartment neat and orderly, laundered, cleaned, cooked, did the shopping and ran errands. She had even found a part time job running a cash register at a nearby convenience store. After her initial uneasiness, Connie discovered she was glad her sister had come, even though it saddened her to see how much of the old fervor for life had not returned.

Sarah had run away from home with her boyfriend while sixteen. Jimmy Nicholson was a charmer, good looking, well spoken, obviously intelligent, but underneath he was petty, cruel, and thoughtless. They were living in Boston when she got pregnant, apparently to her great delight. She wrote to Connie several times, her letters filled with enthusiastic plans for the baby, but never provided a return address.

When she was eight months pregnant, she and Nicholson had a violent argument. He broke her jaw, her nose, and her right arm, and while she was lying unconscious on the floor, he had kicked her repeatedly in the abdomen, then took off, never to be heard from again. Sarah had almost bled to death. She lost the baby and was told that there was no possibility of her ever having another.

Connie still felt her eyes begin to sting whenever she thought about it.

"How'd your day go? Catch any spies?"

"Half a dozen before lunch. Only three in the afternoon. What's for supper?" Connie felt awkward not being able to tell her sister, or anyone else for that matter, about her current assignment, but Sarah didn't seem to resent being kept in the dark.

"Just spaghetti. Sorry, but I didn't have time to do anything more complicated. I was out with Mrs. Wentworth all
day."

"Mrs. Wentworth from downstairs? What's her problem?"

"Cat got out somehow. She was worried sick and she's so frail, I didn't want to let her roam the neighborhood alone. This isn't the best part of town, if you hadn't noticed."

"Did you find it?"

"The cat? Yeah, it was back in her apartment when we gave up. I guess it found a great new place to hide because I looked all over with her before we went out."

Connie felt a sudden, intense pain in the center of her forehead. "What kind of cat is it?"

"Oh, just a tabby."

Rikashi spent three hours the following morning misunderstanding, or deflecting, her questions about the cat. "Life is a continuum, Connie Jensen. Potentiality transcends physical limitations. You must realize this."

"So the cat can be anywhere at all, at any time at all?"

"Only if you realize its existence."

She shook her head with frustration, stretched her arms above her head, glanced back through the last few exchanges, still visible on the screen. Something almost made sense. Rikashi had emphasized several times that she needed to realize the nature of the situation, and she had responded that she was trying to. But suddenly another interpretation suggested itself.   With a few keystrokes, she did a simple search and replace, then sent the transcript to the print queue. As the pages dropped into the bin, she read each in turn, searching for the word "realize", which was now underlined and italicized wherever it appeared.

"Oh my God," she whispered.

"If this is your idea of a joke, Dr. Jensen, I am not amused." Mitchelson slammed his desk drawer shut and turned away, obviously dismissing her. But Colin Kraft spoke up from the corner.

"I'd like to hear her out, Dr. Mitchelson."

"It's not as farfetched as it may sound. Look, no two of us live in the exact same world, and we're human. How can we expect a nonhuman lifeform to do so?"

"We interpret the real world differently, but that doesn't mean there isn't a single objective truth." Mitchelson was still surly, but in deference to Kraft he'd modulated his tone.

"In one sense, perhaps. But a color blind person's vision is just as valid as our own, it just isn't the majority. For some people, chocolate tastes great, or spicy cooking, or broccoli. Some people see the world as a wonderful, beautiful place to live, others as a Darwinian ratrace, still others as a dangerous environment filled with sinister plots and evil forces." She forced herself not to look at Kraft as she said this last. "Each of those interpretations might be equally valid. Rikashi's species realizes how the universe works."

"So you're saying that these aliens know the truth and we don't?"

She shook her head. "You're making the same mistake I did. When Rikashi told me I had to realize the truth, I thought he was criticizing my understanding. But he uses the word 'realize' in the sense of 'making real'. If the laws of the universe aren't absolute, if they're malleable, then perhaps we can pick and choose which of those laws to...to realize."

Mitchelson dismissed her moments later, clearly convinced she'd gone off the deep end. But Kraft remained silent, thoughtful, and Connie wondered if he had more imagination than she'd given him credit for.


"Conversance with the brother of your womb home would be desirable."

Connie stared at the screen thoughtfully. "I have no brother. Do you mean my sister?"

"The one whose greater purple stains your own. Slow tears in the peaceful darkness."

"How do you know about Sarah? I've never mentioned her to you."

"The potential for that knowledge has always existed. It has only now reached realization."

Tumblers clicked in her mind. "I have always had the ability..." she backspaced over the last word and replaced it, "potential to tell you, therefore you possess the knowledge. Is that it?"

"If that is your realization."

She pondered that. "Then why haven't you ever asked me what has happened to your surviving shipmates?"

"Where there is no potential, there is no realization." There was a pause. "Because you will never know what has happened to them."

"And do you?"

"I realize that they will continue. The shape of that continuity has many branches."

"Could you have saved your ship? Could you have prevented it from crashing?"

"Yes." There was a long pause. "But we didn't realize it in time."


Three days later, Rikashi escaped.

Kraft and the security chief, a wafer thin man named Lofton, met Connie in one of the small meeting rooms.

"What's up? I have lots of work to do today."

"I think you'll find your schedule has been altered, Miss Jensen." Lofton stared at a sheaf of papers, never met her eyes.

"That's Doctor Jensen," she said quietly. "Altered how?"

"Have you observed any change in the subject's behavior during the past few days...Doctor Jensen?"

"Nothing in particular. Why?"

Lofton looked stubborn but Kraft seemed to shake himself awake. "We've got a problem, Connie. It escaped about an hour ago."

"It? You mean Rikashi? Escaped? How could he escape from a sealed room?"

Lofton looked uncomfortable, Kraft mildly amused. "A wire burned out in the primary alarm system, and someone spilled coffee onto the backup and shorted it. A few seconds later the magnetic lock on the door malfunctioned for as yet undetermined reasons. The guard at station one was tying his shoelace and looked away from the door for less than ten seconds. The main security monitor burned out and the secondary wasn't live for almost fifteen seconds. The corridor guard was using the restroom and his relief was reading a magazine. Several other minor coincidences contributed as well."

"So he's out of the compound?"

"Yes, it seems so. We thought you might possibly know how he managed all this. The chain of circumstance is, you must admit, extremely unlikely."

"Unlikely," she said slowly, "but possible. And I guess today Rikashi realized how to escape."

The apartment was empty when she got home. Connie picked at some leftovers, too uneasy to eat. Where could Rikashi have gone, and for what reason? She replayed their last several interviews in her mind, searching for some clue, ended up with a headache and no insights.

It was almost ten o'clock. Where was Sarah?

Connie opened the door to the guest room, wondering if her sister had left a note. The room was neat and orderly, no messages in sight, nothing out of place except for something spilled on the rug beside her bed. Sarah crouched, examined the spill. Inch long fibers, tubular, dark.

Rikashi's molted cilia.

Something's happened to Sarah, she realized, then mentally backtracked in a panic. The last thing she should do is realize any such thing. Realizations were dangerous now.

She called Colin Kraft at his emergency number.

Sarah was missing for four days. More of the cilia had been found in the parking lot outside Connie's apartment building, but the trail vanished after that. The existence of Rikashi and his shipmates had not been released to the public, so a variety of cover stories were hastily prepared to justify the exhaustive search that ensued.

On the fourth day following her disappearance, Sarah was found wandering through a small park on the outskirts of Maclean. She was naked and disoriented but apparently uninjured. Connie rushed to the hospital room, was arguing with the security people when Kraft emerged from her sister's room and waved her through.

"She seems to be all right."

She brushed past him without a word. Sarah was awake, alert, and full of questions.

"What's going on, Connie? Who are these people? They act like police but they won't tell me what's going on."

"They're government investigators." Even under stress, Connie's training made her cautious. "How are you feeling? What happened?"

"I don't know. The last thing I remember was trying to decide what to do about supper, and then I had these dreams about...about the baby." She glanced away briefly, then back. "And then some people were putting me in an ambulance and they brought me here. But I feel fine, just confused is all."

They talked further until Connie felt reassured that Sarah was in no physical danger, then excused herself to find a doctor.

She had little luck until Kraft intervened on her behalf.

"Your sister appears to be perfectly fine, Dr. Jensen. We won't know for certain until we have our test results back, but there's no indication of concussion, amnesia, or any physical trauma."

"But she can't remember anything that's happened for the past four days!"

The doctor shrugged. "Perhaps she was drugged. We'll know more when the tests are completed. But I assure you that they're both fine."

"Both?" Connie flashed an absurd scene, Rikashi in a hospital bed while a nurse took his pulse. Pulses, actually.

"Your sister AND the baby," he answered testily.

"Baby? Doctor Weller, my sister isn't pregnant."

"I wasn't aware that your doctorate was in medicine, Dr. Jensen." Weller was openly sarcastic.

"It's not. It's in applied linguistics."

"Then perhaps you'll defer to a specialist. Your sister is very definitely pregnant, about thirty days along, I'd say."

Connie closed her eyes, opened them, spoke as calmly as she could manage. "Dr. Weller, I appreciate our relative positions here. But Sarah was severely injured two years ago. The doctors assured us that she was physically incapable of ever conceiving again. They were quite certain."

He paused only a second. "They were also quite wrong."

But even Dr. Weller expressed amazement when Sarah's records were brought to the hospital by a government courier.

"There must be some mistake. Damage this extensive could not be repaired even surgically, let alone spontaneously. Are you absolutely certain that these are your sister's records?"

Two hours later, they found Rikashi. The alien was lying inside a culvert a quarter mile from where Sarah had been found. There were no apparent life signs and the body had been taken away quickly and quietly.

Sarah drove back to the compound, even though it was nearly midnight. The guard was used to people coming and going at odd hours and buzzed her through without comment. She went straight to her office, called up the transcript files, and began re-reading every conversation she had conducted with Rikashi.

It was daylight when she finished and her brain was spinning with fatigue, and with alarm. She called the hospital, confirmed that there was no change in her sister's situation, and then drove home, fell asleep fully dressed, and didn't wake up until the middle of the afternoon. Awake once more she showered, checked with the hospital again, then called Colin Kraft.

"We need to talk," she said simply. "I'll meet you in your office."

"Are you telling me that the alien raped your sister?"

Connie shook her head. "The purpose of life is life. I don't think Rikashi's species could even grasp the concept of forced procreation."

"But you think it impregnated your sister?"

"In some sense, yes. I think he realized how to repair the damage to her body, then somehow generated life. Whether there is any physical part of him in that life, I just don't know."

"The doctors didn't find anything unusual about the fetus."

"They weren't looking for anything either. But I don't know if there would be any discernible difference. Maybe there won't be until we realize it." She started to laugh, but it sounded hysterical and she stopped quickly.

Kraft remained thoughtful and she was glad he was taking this seriously. She doubted anyone else would. "For the sake of argument, let's say I accept that Rikashi and his kind can alter reality simply by believing they can do it."

"By realizing they can do it," she corrected.

"Whatever. Even if that's possible, humans don't have that ability. And Rikashi is dead."

"Is he?"

Kraft stared at her blankly.

"Life's changes never end," she quoted. "Rikashi's people believe in personal immortality."

"So do Baptists. What's the relevance?"

"I don't think they're as connected to their bodies as we are. They have difficulty interpreting sensory input consistently. They smell sounds or taste colors, neurasthenia. And I found several references in the transcripts to events of which Rikashi could have no direct knowledge."

"Telepathy?"

"I don't think so. I believe that their consciousness is linked to their physical location, but not limited to it."

"I see. Then you think that..." His face twisted into a grimace of distaste.

"No, not think, realize. I realize that Rikashi is still alive, and he's going to be my nephew."

# SPECTERS

If it had been invariably true that opposites attract, Taryn Penshiri and Jeff Marle might have been numbered among history's greatest lovers. In practice, they detested each other with an intensity that was almost tangible. Penshiri was the daughter of first generation settlers, both of whom had died during the Rotting Plague three years after arriving on Lindisfarne, leaving her without anyone to look after her interests. She had been raised in a less than satisfactory, understaffed government orphanage. Marle had been the pampered second son of a family which held substantial investments on most of the dozen worlds humans had been able to colonize. True, he'd been cut off without a credit after his unsuccessful attempt to oust his own father from the Board of Trustees, but he was accustomed to comfort, lived at the limit of his means, and was disinclined to recognize any rules not of his own devising.

Penshiri was serious minded, pragmatic, and organized. Her crawler and all of its equipment was spotless, rigorously and personally checked before each expedition, and she never strayed across the border into territory allotted to the neighboring colony states, even though the wilderness would not even be properly mapped for another generation. Marle paid others to maintain his vehicle, even if that meant straining his credit reserves, and he'd once boasted that he didn't even know where the borders were supposed to run, and certainly didn't feel constrained to observe a prohibition that was virtually unenforceable.

Between trips, Penshiri lived quietly in a modest cottage she'd built for herself on the outskirts of Lavender City, which was barely a town, let alone a city. Marle rented several rooms in one of the tourist centers near the adjacent spaceport. She spent her leisure time painting landscapes and listening to music. He spent his drinking Vitae with contract workers at the technically illegal but generally tolerated underground bars, or visiting Portia's Palace, where you could rent a pleasure partner by the hour or the day. She was short and light boned, but deceptively strong. He was tall, verging on heavy, but his body was surprisingly soft.

They had only two notable commonalities. They both made their living hunting for Spectral artifacts and they were both very good at it.

If there was a specific incident that had ignited their mutual animosity, it was a secret they shared with no one else. Once she'd come of age, Penshiri had methodically saved enough to finance her first trip into the wilderness and she had already discovered three caches by the time Marle arrived on the scene. Despite his disinheritance and his spendthrift ways, he had managed to set aside enough credit to buy himself a first class crawler with all the extras and ensconce himself in an expensive apartment. Another half year passed before he actually set out on his first jaunt into the interior, driven by the rapid decline in his credit level. Penshiri was already among the most successful of the prospectors, a combination of luck and hard work and an instinct for just where the elusive Specters might have left one of their caches behind.

No one expected much from Marle, but he surprised everyone by recovering a nearly intact image recorder during his first trip. The memory module was damaged but technicians had been able to recover some of the holographic imagery, including what was still the most detailed known portrait of an adult Specter. A year later, Marle and Penshiri were consistently earning more than any of their competitors. His detractors said he was damned lucky; her detractors just grumbled inarticulately and insisted that it wasn't fair.

Five years passed during which they were both able to support their respective lifestyles, but their trips were taking longer and their discoveries commanded lesser prices. There was a finite number of caches, after all, and Lavender State had been extensively searched. No one knew a great deal about the Specters - who were not native to Lindisfarne. There were many theories about why they had come, and even more regarding the reason they'd left their caches behind, but no hard evidence. Although their artifacts had been found scattered across every significant landmass, including the polar ice caps, there was no sign of any significant settlement, no cities, no monuments, no industry. They had come to Lindisfarne, explored it thoroughly, and then just stopped coming about two hundred years before humans arrived. There was no hint as to where they'd come from and, so far, no sign of their presence on any other explored world.

Most of the prospectors from Lavender began moving on to Indigo State or newly opened Aquamarine. Penshiri and Marle were not among them. For Penshiri it was a disinclination to leave the home she'd made for herself, for the other it was more likely simple lethargy. Penshiri purchased a license to work in the adjacent state of Tangerine, which meant longer trips, but the landscape there was so difficult to traverse that it remained almost virgin territory. Marle undoubtedly considered a similar course, although naturally he didn't stoop to the formality of obtaining official permission.

So how did I get caught up in the middle of all this? Well, I could tell you all the details, but that's a long and boring story. The short version is that I was desperately trying to acquire some academic credentials in xenoarchaeology and since Lindisfarne was close to my home on Caladon, that's where I was looking. I'd puttered around in the local museums for months, badgering people into letting me examine them closely, but I hadn't realized that all of the really important finds had already been taken offworld for study on Earth, Glissade, and elsewhere. What remained on Lindisfarne were minor pieces and duplicates. I didn't even have enough standing to secure access to new finds before the Caliphate's procurators sold them offworld, splitting the income with the prospectors.

So I considered my options and the sorry state of my credit account and eventually introduced myself to Taryn Penshiri.

We met at a café not far from where she lived. It had taken three calls and considerable groveling before I'd been able to convince her to listen to my offer. I almost didn't recognize her when I arrived; she looks much taller in holos. She was drinking chortleberry tea at a corner table and she barely raised her eyes when I approached and introduced myself.

"Sit down, Mr. Osgood. Would you like some tea?"

It didn't seem possible that this fragile looking, flaxen haired woman, whose head barely reached my shoulder, could possibly be one of the two most successful prospectors on Lindisfarne. Her hands were so small and delicate that she might almost have been a Specter herself, and she spoke so softly that I found myself leaning forward slightly to hear her better, even though the table's filters reduced the background noise to a faint murmur. "Thank you, I would."

She poured from an ornate ceramic pot whose lid was embossed with the café's name, *The Crackpot*. The evening was chilly and the hot liquid was welcome. I sipped slowly, trying to evaluate my companion as surreptitiously as possible. I have no doubt that she was taking my measure as well.

"Have you ever been out in the field before, Mr. Osgood?"

"Not locally, no, but I've worked on Hussein and Shenyang. They're both frontier worlds."

"But both extensively explored. Did you trek in to those sites, or fly?"

"We used lifters in both cases," I admitted. "But I've worked more than once in primitive conditions, Miss Penshiri. And please call me Thaz."

Her face gave nothing away and she didn't offer her own first name in return. "We'd be spending most of our time in a crawler. I have an old model. Technically it's rated for a crew of two, but I use most of the extra space to carry supplies. You're not a small man; it could be very uncomfortable. You would probably be better off with Jeff Marle. He has a four seater with all the modern conveniences."

I'd been on Lindisfarne long enough to know that she and Marle were not friends. I thought about trying to play on that rivalry, but one look at her face warned me off. She'd know what I was doing. "I did try him," I said truthfully. "He turned me down."

Penshiri never blinked, and I wondered if she'd already known that. "So I was your second choice?"

"As you said, he has a roomier vehicle. I gather his last trip was profitable enough that he didn't feel that he needed what I had to offer."

Her lips twitched into the suggestion of a frown. "More likely he didn't want to chance having a witness aboard. Marle tends to disregard the rules." Her tone suggested this should be a capital crime.

"I assure you that my interest is exactly as I've stated. I know when to be discreet."

She looked vaguely offended for a second, then chose to let it pass. "I'll tell you right up front that I don't like doing this. I've worked alone for years now. I enjoy my own company; I like the quiet. I wouldn't even be considering your offer if I had more credit saved up, but I wrecked my primary engine last time out and I had to bring in a new one from offworld. Your stipend will cover the expenses of this trip, just barely, if we come up empty, and there's always a chance of that. I can't promise you any return on your investment."

I felt a glow of elation. I'd been hopeful ever since she'd agreed to meet with me, but there had remained the chance that she'd turn me down. "I understand the situation. I'll do my best to stay out of your way."

"How much equipment do you intend to bring?"

"Just a small personal bag, a recorder, and a test kit." I was already mentally sorting through my meager belongings, deciding what I should take. "How long will we be away?"

She shrugged. "Best case scenario is thirty days, but it's never that easy. Normally I'd have a ninety day operating window, but with you along, no more than sixty. By then we'll be low on supplies, unless one of us cracks and kills the other first, of course."

I laughed uncomfortably. Her expression never changed.

We left three days later, traveling by lifter to a clearing she'd scouted on a previous trip. The pilot watched us back out of the cargo bay, waved perfunctorily, and was airborne within seconds. I felt suddenly very far from civilization.

Penshiri hadn't been kidding about the cramped quarters. The passenger compartment had been shifted forward to increase the cargo space, leaving just enough room to accommodate her comfortably. I couldn't stretch my legs out no matter what position I assumed, and I was constantly shifting my knees from one side to the other to keep my legs from cramping. Whenever we hit anything but the most gentle of bumps, my head banged against the roof, and I ended up hunching my shoulders to minimize the number of lumps on my skull. Despite the efforts of the suspension system to keep us level, the ride was so bumpy that I gave up attempting to write in my journal except when we were stopped for meals or at night.

And that was the easiest part of the journey because for the first two days we traveled across relatively smooth terrain, open fields, game trails, and briefly along a shallow streambed. On the third morning we turned onto what Penshiri called the Runagate Trail. If there was a trail, it was invisible to me, but she never hesitated, picking her way across a hilly countryside pockmarked with patches of broccoli trees and occasional crumbling boulders. I had offered to drive a couple of times, but she had always refused to relinquish control, and now it would have been impractical.

I should mention something about the sleeping arrangements. It was possible to sleep, sitting up, in the cab of the crawler, but whenever I tried even a nap in that position, I woke up with a sore back, a stiff neck, and other aches and pains. Penshiri had a Safetent that could hold two comfortably, but she'd insisted that I bring along one of my own.

She had made her feelings on the matter amply clear the night before our departure. At her request, I'd met her at one of the dingier bars on the fringe of the spaceport. We had just ordered our second round of drinks when a heavy set man wearing a Mercantilist uniform had made a crude suggestion. I had pretended not to hear, but Penshiri responded with a particularly obscene insult. The Mercantilist stalked over to our table, shouting incoherent threats, and she'd risen to meet him, moving so quickly that I never saw exactly what happened. It ended, almost immediately, with the Mercantilist lying on the floor, nursing a broken arm.

"We can go now," she'd said quietly, not even breathing hard. I had received the message loud and clear.

I was hopelessly lost but Penshiri assured me we were on course for the border with Tangerine. "We'll head up the Ramble River to the Wandering Islands and then see what looks good."

The Wandering Islands were a series of sandbars formed where the Upper Ramble and the Big Torrent converged. They were constantly appearing and disappearing, changing contours, as the violent currents intertwined. The coastland on both sides was similarly elastic, alternately eroding and being buttressed by silt. The border between Tangerine and Lavender was none too precise in this area, but since Penshiri was licensed for both, that wasn't an issue.

Although I'd intended to honor her preference for peace and quiet, I'm a hopelessly sociable person and by the third day I was tentatively trying to draw her out. Occasionally she responded to my conversational gambits, often with shrugs or monosyllables, sometimes more expressively. It was clear that she didn't want to talk about her personal life, but she'd open up a bit more about her work, and on one occasion became positively expansive on the subject of the Specters.

"They were tourists, not settlers," she insisted.

I'd counter argued, citing authorities who insisted that Lindisfarne was a failed colony.

"Settlers build settlements," she'd answered, as though that was all the refutation that was necessary. "The Specters came here to observe and enjoy, not to change things. That's why it's so hard to locate their caches. If you weren't looking for them, you wouldn't know they were there. Do you realize how little variation we've found in what they left behind? It's as if they all brought pretty much the same luggage."

"For all we know, the stuff they left behind was a basic survival kit," I pointed out. "The first wave of colonists on Lindisfarne probably all carried pretty much the same equipment."

"I'll grant you the sleeping bowls are pretty rudimentary, but what about the music balls?"

Speculation was that the Specters were able to alter their own skeletal structure, if they had skeletons. We weren't sure; we'd never found any physical remains. Some of the images that had survived had shown Specters resting in the perfectly circular bowls which were found in almost every cache, but they were very foreshortened versions of the eerie figures we'd seen represented elsewhere. Specters looked almost like humans with cloaks, full skirts, and fringed blouses, until you realized that they didn't wear clothing. All those frills and folds were flesh. Superficially they resembled some of the local lifeforms, particularly the Banshees, but so far no one had found anything to suggest they'd evolved on Lindisfarne. The most popular theory contended that they'd chosen this world for whatever it is that they were doing here because it resembled wherever they'd come from.

The sleeping bowls were probably a basic utilitarian device in which the Specters rested between periods of activity. The music balls, on the other hand, were translucent spheres riddled with passageways, each of which was fitted with a thin reed. During the windy season, a music ball placed outside would produce a strange blend of sounds that some claimed to find soothing. Most authorities believed they served a recreational or artistic purpose, but for all we

42

knew, they were really some kind of bug zapper and the sleeping bowls were toilets.

"I just don't think we have enough hard data to draw any firm conclusions." Professing ignorance is a weak defense, but in this case it was all I could manage.

She made a noise that said quite eloquently that she considered her own theory irrefutable.

On the seventh day, we entered a swampy region filled with rotting tree stumps. There was a storm during the afternoon and lightning must have struck nearby because we were forced to divert around a sizeable forest fire. That meant spending the night in the swamp or continuing to move in the darkness. Penshiri considered the matter and announced we would wait until morning.

"We'll have to sleep inside."

I glanced around. It wasn't the prettiest piece of real estate I'd seen, but there was a patch of relatively bare, dry ground not far away. "What about over there? We could pitch at least one tent."

"You think so?" She opened the door on her side and stepped down from the cab. I followed suit and met her at the crawler's nose, walking carefully along the edge of our treads to keep my feet dry. The treads consisted of interlocking components like chain mesh, all connected by an electronic neuroweb that evaluated conditions under the entire vehicle, compensating for weight distribution, irregularities in the surface, anything else that might affect our progress. It wouldn't climb a cliff or cross an ocean, but it could handle almost any other surface. The treads were splayed grotesquely at the moment, balancing on islands of semi-solid soil, pools of thick mud, and occasional patches of open water.

I started to pick my way across to the place I'd noticed but Penshiri caught me by the arm. "Wait." She looked around, found a tuberous plant growing nearby, bent forward and yanked it out by the roots. My stomach churned as the thick white root she'd pulled from the soil writhed and twisted, trying to wriggle free, but she never gave it a second glance. Instead, she tossed it, underhand, across the narrow gap. It landed on my chosen camp site, rolled over once, then began burrowing itself into the ground.

Unfortunately, that place was already taken. A dozen or more thin, ropy tentacles thrust themselves up out of the loose soil in a rough circle around the newcomer. It was tangled in them almost immediately and, after what could not have been much more than a few seconds, all movement had ceased. "Sandwraith nest," said Penshiri. "They have a hell of a sting. Sometimes even a Safetent won't keep them out."

My revulsion must have shown on my face because she laughed at me. "Life is a constant struggle against death, Osborn. Better get used to it."

So we spent the night in the crawler. Penshiri was small enough that she could curl up in her seat in something like a natural sleeping position. I wasn't nearly as fortunate, but after I'd endured an hour of twisting and turning, she took pity and showed me how to rearrange some of our supplies so that I could recline the seat partway and achieve something approximating comfort.

A flock of banshees passed us a little later. I'd seen these diaphanous creatures before, but never in large numbers. Out here in the middle of nowhere, they drifted overhead in loose formations of twenty or more, their long sticky tendrils sifting flying insects from the air, translucent mantles streaming behind like a para-sail to help keep them aloft. Their low, mournful cries seemed almost human, which was amusing when you were watching them in a preserve near the settlement, but downright spooky under our current circumstances. Local folklore said that when the Specters abandoned the planet, some of their number were left behind and became the Banshees, but it was obvious nonsense. Banshees had a surprisingly sophisticated nervous systems but their evolution from much smaller indigenous ancestors was well established.

I couldn't relax until they were gone, but Penshiri glanced around once to see what was up, then went immediately back to sleep. She was not a type I normally found attractive, but our situation and the close proximity played havoc with my hormones. I was about to reach across to her when I remembered the Mercantilist with the broken arm, and probably saved myself a similar injury.

We began searching in earnest the following morning, each of us wrapped up in our own thoughts. Although we had a radio, Penshiri never called in and only occasionally listened to newscasts from the capital. There were now three supply ships overdue and the Caliphate was temporarily rationing certain imported goods like dietary supplements. The Free Traders and the Empiricals were rattling sabers again, so it was likely that the merchant ships were delaying their departure until both sides grew tired of posturing. It was a cycle we'd seen before. Back when we first reached the stars, optimists foresaw a period when people could just move on if they didn't like their government, an era of live and let live. The pessimists figured we'd just take our longstanding animosities into space and work them out on a bigger scale. Guess who turned out to be right.

Penshiri wasn't very forthcoming when I asked her how she identified a probable site, and I soon realized she was protecting her personal trade secrets. Somehow she had learned how to predict, or at least increase the probability of predicting, the location of a Spectral cache. That afternoon we actually found one, but it had already been emptied by one of her competitors. It was a small chamber built into the side of a gentle slope, and I was dumbfounded when she leaned forward, inserted three fingers into what appeared to be a clump of grass, and pulled open the door to an unlighted compartment about the size of a closet.

I watched her poke around at three more locations that day, and six on the day following, but no additional chambers revealed themselves. We crossed a good sized stream and turned to follow the opposite shore. "They liked waterways," she explained. "As long as they flowed north to south."

"What's wrong with east to west?"

She shrugged. "You're studying them. You tell me."

Two days later, we found two caches during the same morning. The first was empty, but the second was untouched. We had to dig with our shovels for a few minutes before we could open the door, but the interior of the ceramic chamber was immaculate. I watched as Penshiri recovered a very nice, medium sized sleeping bowl, several featureless glass balls, something that looked like a series of printed circuits attached to a metal bar, and a very handsome and well preserved pennant. We don't know what purpose the pennants served, but that's exactly what they were, decorated with symbols or patterns or both. A family crest, perhaps. Or maybe individual Specters had unique pennants. As far as I know, no others have yet been found.

It wasn't a particularly large cache, but Penshiri was obviously pleased with herself, even deigned to smile a bit, and told me how she was going to spend the bounty. "I'm going to have the backup power unit reconditioned, and redo the integrated circuits on the treads. If there's anything left after that, I'll add another layer of undercoating. She was clearly pleased with her plans. I thought it all sounded pretty dull. What good was finding a treasure if you only used the reward to help find more treasure?

Her mood soured slowly over the next three days, during which time we found nothing at all. She was so dour that I'd even stopped trying to initiate a conversation, and I was taken a bit aback when she uncharacteristically volunteered some information late on the third day. "We're close to the Wanderers. We should see them some time tomorrow."

I thought by then that I understood at least some of the physical characteristics common to all the sites she'd searched. Each had been well shaded, situated on slightly inclining ground, and faced toward the planetary equator. There were probably other indications that I missed, because we passed up many places that met those criteria. Clearly she had some sort of insight relative to the Specters, however murky, and I made careful notes. As far as I was aware, no research had ever been conducted among the prospectors to determine if there were observable behavioral differences between those who were successful and those who failed.

We camped that night inside a circle of yinyan trees, whose interlocking trunks were so tightly fit except for one narrow gap that it was almost as though we were indoors. Penshiri was more talkative than usual, though hardly garrulous; she was obviously looking forward to the morning. "I came up this way years ago, but I was new then and I might have missed a lot of places that would be obvious now."

She surprised me then by changing the subject to something she'd refused to talk about earlier. Her family. "My mother would have loved it out here. Dad was a bit of a stick in the mud. Our farm was the world to him, all the world he needed anyway. But Mom had an itchy foot and a bit of the gypsy in her blood. I think she's the one who talked him into coming out here, to Lindisfarne I mean." She hesitated for a few seconds. "It killed them both, I suppose, but it's part of who she was."

Those few words seemed to have softened her somehow, and I shifted position self-consciously, closing the gap between us. She glanced at me, her eyes cool, and then ostentatiously moved away, restoring the previous distance. It was like a slap in the face and I felt angry and embarrassed. A few minutes later, she stood up and went to her tent, sealing it behind her. I sat up a while longer, then crawled into my own.

We reached the Wanderers about mid-day. They were low and mostly featureless, although some of the older ones had vegetation, low grass or skeletal bushes and small trees. Many were polished smooth and from a distance looked like the backs of leviathans rising from the depths to sun themselves. It had been rainy in the mountains and water levels were high. Penshiri stayed close to the riverbed, taking advantage of the easier terrain, so I had a pretty good view. They were interesting for an hour or so, but I'd already begun to lose interest by the time we reached the ford.

Theoretically, crawlers can cross rivers, compensating for the current, but it was always a tricky business. I kept my mouth shut without being told; the intensity of Penshiri's concentration was all the warning I needed. I confess that I felt a stir of panic when the water closed overhead. Penshiri had increased the interior air pressure but we had a leak anyway, a pinhole that spurted water hard enough to sting. She slid a marker across the console toward me without moving her eyes away from the fluctuating indicators on her drive board. "Mark that so we can fix it tonight."

It seemed to take forever, but we were actually submerged less than five minutes. My right side was completely soaked, but I'd managed to inscribe a circle around the leak. The crawler lumbered up the opposite bank and headed inland.

"Is this still Lavender or are we in Tangerine now?"

"That depends on who settles here first, I guess. We're on a sliver of land below Lake Sienna and between the rivers. The border is kind of a dotted line here."

We reached the lake an hour later. On the far side, I could just make out a magnificent series of waterfalls. When we stopped to eat and stretch our legs, we heard a faint murmuring in the distance. Clouds of mist rose from the turbulent water. Penshiri seemed to know where she was going, but when I raised the subject she shrugged and I had to be satisfied with a vague answer. Either she didn't want to tell me or, more likely, she was working on instinct.

We stayed a safe distance from the falls, but the roar of the falling water was audible even inside the insulated crawler. It wasn't a straight drop but a series of steps, actually several parallel series of steps. From a distance the water appeared to fall in thick veils, sometimes intersecting one another. From close at hand, it was a seething, foaming, roaring chaos. The thundering and shaking was so constant that it began to seem normal, so I was taken completely by surprise when Penshiri, made a sharp turn, cut the engines, and came to a stop in an open area protected by a flare of stone that served as an enormous umbrella.

"We walk from here."

Well, it was an incline and it was shady, so I suppose it fit those few criteria I'd tentatively identified. Theoretically I was helping with the search, but I noticed that the pattern she laid out for us ensured that she revisited almost every place on my section of the grid. I didn't blame her. The caches we'd seen earlier in the trip had all been completely invisible to me, even from close at hand. But I made an effort. Sitting in the crawler for most of the trip hadn't done much for my stamina, though, and within an hour the backs of my thighs were cramped and I had a mild backache. I surreptitiously swallowed a painkiller while Penshiri was out of sight.

There was a lot of ground to cover and we didn't finish before dark. We camped there that night, our tents side by side. We were barely five steps apart but there might as well have been a continent between us. I had been disabused of any thoughts of flirtation and I was too sore and tired to have initiated anything even if she'd been receptive.

We found the cache early the next morning. I say "we", but of course it was Penshiri who found it. I'm happy to say it was not in a grid square that I'd been responsible for. The terrain behind the falls was as rugged as anything on Lindisfarne. The mountains rose sharply here, with only a suggestion of foothills. Even to my inexperienced eye I could tell that a pretty massive chunk of land had been violently folded along an almost straight line. The barrier was so sharply delineated that it could almost have been artificial.

We had picked our way across a half dozen minor landslides by now. I was enough of a geologist to recognize quartz and feldspar, and the distinct lines of color on the exposed cliff faces were obviously sedimentary. Darker soil appeared only in the more sheltered areas, and it was here that we concentrated. It had grown chilly and I would have preferred to remain out in the sunlight, but Penshiri spent little time where there was no shade.

I was poking around a thick patch of low brush when I heard her calling. She was standing out in the open, hands on her hips, staring up into a deep, shadowy cleft. "Tell me what you see," she ordered.

The small trees and vines were significantly larger here, which suggested it had been stable for a long time. I said so and she nodded approvingly, which pleased me disproportionately. "Does anything strike you as unusual?"

I took my time, squinting in an attempt to pierce the shadows in the deeper recesses. "Not really," I confessed. She made a mildly reproving sound and directed my attention to the shape of the cleft, the regularity of its outline.

"The back wall is the same shape as the opening. That's a pretty big coincidence, don't you think?"

I followed her into the cleft, and it was like stepping from one world into another. Not only was it darker, but the background noise of the waterfall was dramatically reduced. I felt as though I was walking into the Grand Mosque back in Lavender City, or the Universalist Cathedral on Caladon. I had trouble focusing my eyes in the gloom, but even if it had been bright and sunny, I doubt I would have noticed anything. Penshiri had no such problem. "There's something here, all right. Come look."

I joined her, and when she pointed, I was able to see what had roused her interest, a lighter patch in the darkness. "Isn't that…?"

"Yes," she punched me in the arm. "It's part of a cache cover. An undisturbed one." She brushed away some of the soil, exposing more of the cover's edge. "This is the bottom right corner. The rest of it's pretty well buried though. We'll need tools."

"No, you won't." The voice came from behind, flat, unemotional, and cool. Needless to say, it was Jeff Marle who stood there, with a shovel resting on one shoulder.

The cleft had been a quiet, peaceful place, but in that instant it became charged with a tension so electric that I could almost feel the hairs stirring on my forearms.

Penshiri turned to face him, but stayed where she was. "What are you doing here, Marle? You're not licensed to work in

Tangerine." I'd heard irritation in her voice before, but nothing like this.

"Technically, no, I'm not. But technically, this isn't Tangerine. The border hereabouts is unresolved." Marle's tone was artificially light, as though he couldn't be bothered to react to Penshiri's hostility.

"Wherever we are, I'm not about to let you take away my claim."

"YOUR claim? Who do you think uncovered part of it so that you could find it in the first place?"

"I already knew it was here."

He smiled. "But I was here first, so why don't you and your boyfriend just move along?"

"I'm not her boyfriend." I don't think either of them even heard my attempt to clarify my position.

"You have to open the cache to claim it, Marle."

Marle took the shovel off his shoulder and gestured with it. "Exactly what I had in mind."

There was a subtle change in Penshiri's stance. I blinked and recognized it. The last time she'd been in that position, a drunken Mercantilist had suffered a broken arm. "You're not stealing my claim, Marle."

Marle hesitated only for a second, then gripped the shovel with both hands. "It's not your claim, Penshiri. And I won't be frightened off by a hot-headed mudgee." A mudgee is a tiny carrion eater. It was not a term of endearment. Penshiri took a deliberate step forward and Marle's hand tightened on the shovel handle.

"Now wait a minute," I said hastily, but to no effect. Once again, I don't think they even heard me. There were a couple more exchanges of insults and the gap between them had been cut in half before I finally shouted at them, more exasperated than anything else.

"Shut up! Both of you!"

They heard me this time, and their heads turned in my direction. Marle's expression made my blood run cold. Penshiri's froze it in my veins. I pushed on before they could react and before I lost my nerve. "There's got to be some way to settle this without threats or violence."

Penshiri looked as though she didn't recognize me at first, but then she smiled, the smile of a dawncat about to pounce on a fuzzilope. "That's right. We have a witness, Marle. I guess you're outnumbered."

Marle pursed his lips. "Not necessarily. Who are you anyway?"

"Thaz Osborn. I'm a research scientist." It was only a bit of an exaggeration. "I spoke to you a few weeks back."

He nodded. "That's right. I remember now. You're self financed, aren't you?"

"At the moment," I admitted.

"Well, how would you like to earn enough to outfit your own expedition?"

To my credit, I think, I didn't immediately realize what he was suggesting. Penshiri was quicker on the uptake. "You slimey dungworm! You're trying to bribe him to lie for you!"

He rounded on her. "I'm trying to reward him for telling the truth. I found it first. It belongs to me!"

They were closer now, almost within arm's reach. "I'm not lying for anyone!" I thought about stepping between them, then thought again. "Listen! Neither of you has a legitimate claim until the cache is opened, right?"

They both nodded but neither looked in my direction.

"Then why don't we work together and clear it off. Then I'll open the cache and the two of you can divide up whatever we find."

I didn't think they were going to buy it, and it took some more talking before they grudgingly accepted a convoluted plan. Marle would split the artifacts into two piles, and then Penshiri would have first choice. They both insisted that I make a recorded statement relinquishing all rights to the contents of the cache, since technically they belonged to me if I opened the lid. They both took copies of the recording and transmitted them to their brokers before they'd proceed. I felt like I was mediating between a pair of children, or between the Free Traders and the Empiricals.

We spent most of the remaining daylight clearing off the cache. Because it was set well back in a recess, the wind that blew stray dirt and debris in rarely cleared any of it back out. The cache lid was even bigger than we'd estimated, three times the width of the largest previously known, and tall enough that we had difficulty clearing off the top. When we were finally done, shadows had crept in all around us as though we stood in a patch of night, looking back out into the day.

"We'll need lights," said Marle. Penshiri nodded without speaking. It was the first time I'd seen her physically exhausted since I'd met her. We fetched lamps from the crawlers and set them in a semicircle.

Now that it was time to open the cache, I felt strangely reluctant to do so. Penshiri and Marle weren't being cordial to each other, but the overt hostility had disappeared. "What are you waiting for?" she asked finally, but without rancor.

Theoretically I knew how the cache lids worked, but I'd never actually operated the mechanism before. I inserted my fingers into the opening of the bottom right hand corner. It felt odd, obviously not made for a human hand, but after wiggling my fingers a bit I felt a slight movement within the mechanism. There was a faint puff of air and the cover swung open of its own accord.

I don't know what I was expecting to see. The first thing I recognized was a sleeping bowl, lying on the floor of the cache directly in front of me. It was perfectly ordinary, except that it contained at least a half dozen music balls, and that had never happened before. Then my eyes trailed up and I saw more bowls, dozens of them, set on shelf-like ledges that ran from floor to ceiling. Each of the bowls contained more of the balls. There must have been hundreds of them.

I was vaguely aware of my two companions brushing past me. The cache was deeper than I expected, large enough that we could all fit comfortably inside. Behind the double row of sleeping bowls were more items, some that I recognized – flying recorders, other devices that were known to sense the planet's magnetic fields but whose purpose we could only guess at, sheets of delicate netting or filters. There were also objects which were completely new to me, including unions of electronics and ceramics, pyramid shaped objects all of whose faces were mirrors, and so on. Marle and Penshiri were like kids in a toy shop; I think they even briefly forgot that they didn't like each other.

They spent the evening completing a joint inventory. It was obvious that an even split was going to be simpler than they expected. Then an argument started about whether it would be better to cash in the whole find at once, or sell them over a period of months or even years so that the prices would not drop as precipitately. By the time we quit for the night, they were at each other's throats again, and neither would leave until they'd erected a dual coded proximity alarm in front of the cache, so that no one could cheat in the darkness.

We did encounter an unexpected problem the following morning, or rather, Penshiri did. Although Marle's crawler had adequate free space for his share, it was pretty obvious that Penshiri did not. She started going through her equipment and supplies, throwing out bulky items that would be easy to replace, cutting our food stores until we had just enough to see us back to the pickup point. At one point I caught her looking at me speculatively, and I thought she was trying to decide whether or not I could be jettisoned, but she sighed and turned away and I felt relatively safe. Actually, even with his share fully loaded, there was ample space in Marle's vehicle for a passenger, and I broached the subject. Penshiri obviously didn't like the idea and sacrificed more of her equipment until she had sufficient space. I didn't flatter myself that it was because she enjoyed my company; she just didn't trust the two of us together out of her hearing.

All of this consumed another day and by the time everything was loaded, they were too tired to carp at each other, and I wasn't happy with either of them, so we ate our evening meal in relative peace. Penshiri even listened to a newscast for a while, which is how we heard that the *Abelard* had finally appeared in orbit, three months late. They hadn't sent their shuttle down yet, but the spaceport authority reported that the cargo ship was badly damaged, possibly from an internal explosion.

Neither of my companions showed any interest in the cache once it was empty, so I made my final visit alone. I had already taken extensive recordings of the contents and the empty interior, but I wanted one final look around before we left. It was dusk and the light was bad so it was pretty close to a miracle that I found something we'd previously overlooked. The cache tapered slightly so that the rear wall was the same shape but about twenty percent smaller than the opening. Cache doors all open outward, and the control is invariably located in the lower right hand corner.

There was a control inset in the rear wall, on the lower left hand corner, partially concealed by the shadow of one of the shelves.

I crouched and stared, using my torchlight to examine it from every angle. Then I reached out and inserted my fingers, tugging slightly. It didn't move at first. You have to exert pressure in just the right way. But a minute or two of experimentation bore fruit, there was the sudden sound of air pressure equalizing, and the rear wall of the cache opened. Inward. Cache doors always opened outward.

I suppose I was expecting another store room, but my light revealed only a good sized chamber cut directly into the hill, with an unadorned pedestal in the center of the room. The pedestal was large enough that I could have climbed up onto it if the top surface hadn't been completely encased in a tall dome of some transparent substance that might have been glass or even a very hard plastic. I stood frozen for a while, then slowly entered the inner chamber, flashing my light around what turned out to be an oval room about ten meters across the longer axis. The walls were absolutely featureless and believe me, I examined them very closely this time. When I was satisfied that the pedestal was the only artifact, I turned my attention there.

There were three steps descending from the pedestal on one side, but if there was a way to open the glass dome without breaking it, I never figured it out. There wasn't the hint of a seam anywhere. Around the circumference of the base I found three more locking devices, each of which opened to reveal compartments containing recognizable Spectral ceramo-circuitry, although of a complexity beyond anything I'd seen or read about. More significantly, when I reached out, the hairs on the back of my hand stirred and rose. This was not a discarded or inoperable piece of equipment; it was still powered on.

Penshiri called my name from somewhere in the distance and I hastily retreated into the first compartment, closing the door to the inner cache. It wasn't avarice that made me decide not to tell the others what I'd found. I was afraid that they'd do something to jeopardize the integrity of the pedestal, perhaps cut it in half according to the terms of their agreement. I couldn't let that happen because the potential loss to science was incalculable. Although I had no proof, I was certain that I had found a clue to the means by which the Specters had come and gone from Lindisfarne, and I wasn't about to let the secret be compromised. I would say nothing until I returned, then contact Professor Goebling on Caladon. With his help, I would lead an expedition back here to study the pedestal where it stood, and perhaps unravel a secret that would revolutionize space travel. I believed that the pedestal was the terminus for a system of matter transmission.

"We thought you'd gotten lost," said Penshiri when I returned to our encampment. She didn't sound particularly concerned.

We left the following morning. I was initially surprised to hear that Penshiri and Marle had agreed to use her pickup site and travel there together, but then I figured that they didn't trust one another enough to let the other out of sight, although I couldn't figure out how either of them could renege on their deal at this point. Or maybe they'd decided that there was always a chance that some misfortune could overtake the other, leaving the survivor in possession of both halves of their booty.

Penshiri tried to contact the lifter pilot and set up a rendezvous, but there was no reply. Then she turned on the radio to catch up on the news and all we heard was static. That wasn't too alarming; the Caliphate had minimized expenses by importing a lot of previously owned equipment and outages were not uncommon. We didn't start to get worried until the blackout continued into the second day, and then the third, and by then we knew that the entire communications network was down.

I won't bore you with the details of how we made our way back to Lavender City. We were able to forage a bit to supplement our dwindling supplies, but it took five weeks to reach the outskirts of the capital and we were all pretty hungry by then, even Marle, who'd refused to share his disproportionately large stock of provisions. The fires were mostly out when we arrived. The damage could have been worse; the robot missile had taken out most of the commercial district, but the farms were almost untouched. We never did find out which side was responsible. The Caliphate had remained neutral, playing the Free Traders and Empiricals against each other. Trying to make friends with both had resulted in succeeding with neither.

Marle disappeared during one of the waves of riots a couple of months later, and is probably buried in one of the mass graves. Penshiri died defending her cottage from looters. I've managed to survive by keeping a low profile and staying away from the trouble spots. I never did find out what happened to all the Spectral artifacts we brought back. With offworld contact severed – we haven't seen a ship in over two years now – the market for them is gone. No one locally has time to spend studying alien artifacts; it's hard enough just to stay alive. Theoretically, Lindisfarne was self sufficient, with a population of about a quarter of a million. We're probably down to a third of that now, and still dropping steadily.

Local news has to travel by word of mouth, and it's hard to separate rumor from fact, but stories have been spreading that the Specters are back. They haven't come anywhere near what used to be Lavender City, at least as far as I know, but travelers and refugees insist that they've been seen singly and in small groups. I wouldn't be at all surprised. I think they only stayed away because we were here. Humans, I mean. And I don't think we'll be here for much longer.

Obviously I'll never know exactly what it was that I found out there. I'm no longer convinced that it was a matter transmitter. How would the Specters have known to stop coming here just two hundred years before we arrived? That's an eye blink in historical terms. It might have been coincidence, but if so, why did they choose to come back now, if they really have?

So I have a new theory, and I don't talk about it because it would sound crazy, and crazy people have a tendency to die suddenly. Those of us who survived the riots and the short lived People's State watch each other closely for any signs of instability. Extraordinary behavior could be a warning of violence, so we are pre-emptively violent in our own defense.

But here, in my journal, I can speak as I wish, and if I'm losing my mind, then there's no one to know. You see, I think the Specters ARE related to the banshees, that they ARE native to Lindisfarne. The banshees are their primitive ancestors, and they've come back from some unimaginably remote future, perhaps to study their own evolution. Or maybe it's too honor the past or even just to satisfy their curiosity. And somehow they knew about humanity's brief invasion, and they carefully avoided us because in the long run, we made no difference in their history, we came and went very quickly.

I imagine we're long gone by their time and I wonder if we still exist in their legends, if we have become frightening creatures from their past, and if there are still stories that we might someday return from the dead. Like ghosts. Like specters.

# BOOK DAY

Evan took his time getting bathed and dressed. It was his personal Book Day and he was feeling a little bit anxious. It wasn't that he didn't look forward to the ceremony – it was after all another sign that he had become an adult – but like many people his age, he still had trouble making his final decision. He'd narrowed it down, of course, and there were only three remaining possibilities, but he was terribly afraid that he was going to make the wrong choice, and that would bother him even though he would never actually know that his judgment had been faulty.  And the last three possibilities varied so dramatically that in many ways they were not directly comparable.

He still lived with his family despite having reached his majority, but they'd already gone ahead. It was customary for each individual to make his or her own way on Book Day, to underscore their new independence, to demonstrate that they were capable of making choices that would have repercussions lasting a life time. His mother had left him an assortment of pastries and fruit and there was fresh coffee. He took his time over breakfast, but not too much time. He didn't want to be late for one of the most important events in his life, a day that would in subtle and unforeseeable ways shape his entire future.

Evan had his own car, but his parents had rented the Knights of Magellan Hall only six blocks away because it was large enough and convenient so he decided to walk. For some reason he was seeing the neighborhood with new eyes this morning, and that vision would almost certainly change again within a few hours.

As he drew near, he could tell by the number of vehicles in the parking lot that most of the guests had already arrived at the hall. All of his relatives would be here, of course, plus friends and co-workers from the Ebay Shopping Center security office. Evan hesitated a few seconds, then walked inside and found himself shaking hands with people he hadn't seen for years and others he spoke to virtually every day. Almost everyone acted as though they were seeing him in an entirely different fashion than they had previously, although it was Evan who would soon have the new perspective. The

Publications Conservation Officer was there as well, sitting on the small stage beside his equipment, attempting to look interested even though he probably attended similar ceremonies several times every week. Everyone was required to have a book day within three months of their eighteenth birthday.

The seating arrangements accommodated the crowd with no difficulty but the display area was so congested that only a handful of people could pass through at any given time. Evan had always been a reader, convinced that each new book he opened would surpass everything he'd read before. Temporary shelving had been set up in tightly packed parallel rows, and every shelf was completely filled with the books he'd read as a child and young adult. Theoretically they were arranged chronologically and some effort had been made to segregate childhood classics from contemporary fiction, but Evan had also done considerable re-reading and a strict progression was impossible to define. All but three of his books – the final three - were there, the missing titles having been moved to an elaborately decorated table on the stage, where he would soon step forward to make his final decision.

Evan made a circuit of the room, accepting congratulations, asking after cousins he'd not seen in months, nodding at answers he wasn't really hearing. The impending decision pushed aside all other thoughts. Eventually he decided that he had greeted everyone who needed to be acknowledged, and a glance at the clock mounted over the exit told him that he needed to move things along. With a last look around, as though expecting to see his childhood lurking in some corner of the room, he walked up onto the stage.

As was customary, he and the PCO were alone on the platform. Evan had prepared a little speech, long enough that the guests wouldn't feel cheated, short enough that they wouldn't get restless. He talked about the three books in question, each of which he'd read multiple times, and how great an impression they had made on his development and life choices. One was a light but witty comedy that always cheered him up, even when he'd been grieving for the loss of his younger sister, run down by a drunk driver. One was a story of human striving, of triumph in the face of great adversity, an uplifting novel that filled him with optimism about what he and the human race might accomplish. The third was a densely serious work that he had not particularly enjoyed when he'd first read it. But months later he'd found himself thinking about questions it had raised and he'd read it again, and over the next three years he'd been drawn back to it repeatedly. Each new visit had revealed insights into human nature that he'd previously missed.

He paused, then drew a deep breath. And because he had learned something new each time he read the third book, he told the audience, that would be the one he chose on his Book Day.

There was general applause and a sudden stirring behind him as the PCO, who'd become increasingly restless, readied the equipment. Evan waited for the crowd to settle down, waved to his parents, and walked over to the PCO. "What do I do?" It was an unnecessary question. He'd attended a dozen Book Days as a spectator and the procedure never varied. But somehow, standing on the stage himself, it felt different.

"Just take a seat. Make yourself comfortable. This will only take a moment and I promise it doesn't hurt a bit."

Obediently, Evan seated himself, and even though he knew the process was painless, he felt a tremor of apprehension as the helmet was secured on his head. There was no other physical sensation, no electric shock even when the power was turned on and the machine began to hum to itself. Evan closed his eyes, fell into a daydream as the soothing effect spread through his mind. "Just concentrate on your selection. The sensors can read your intentions pretty well, but sometimes they slip up if your thoughts wander at the wrong moment. You wouldn't want to have to go through all this again, would you?"

"No, sir." Sally McCullough had requested a resetting. It was considered gauche and there was a substantial penalty charge. She had waited until the last minute to request it as well, and if they hadn't been able to work her in before the statutory limit expired, she would have been stuck with the wrong choice. Evan concentrated furiously on the book he'd chosen.

Time passed, only a few seconds, and then there was a click and the helmet was lifted away. "All done," said the PCO, smiling brightly.

Evan stood up, feeling different without knowing yet just what that difference was. The PCO handed him a book, one of three on the table. He had no recollection of ever having seen it before. Nor could he recall anything about the other two, or any of the hundreds on the shelves arranged around the room, books which would shortly be carted off to a Dispersion Center for distribution to younger readers.

Attached to the volume in his hand was a small electronic device. He recognized it and remembered how it worked. He was excited about the prospect of trying it. As soon as he could gracefully leave, he would walk home and read this marvelous book that he had chosen for reasons he could no longer remember. He would experience it as if it was the first time he'd ever read it, and then he'd press the device to his head, activate it, and all memory of the book's contents would vanish from his mind. This would be his book, and for the rest of his life, he could rediscover it for the first time, over and over again, secure in the knowledge that it would always be a new and rewarding experience.

Thanks to the advent of Book Day, it was no longer necessary to publish new works of fiction. So much existed already that there was certainly an optimal book for every individual reader. It was just a matter of finding the right one before reaching your eighteenth birthday.

As soon as Evan got home, he began reading his book. It was a little difficult at first, but he knew he'd enjoy it eventually.

# NEIGHBOR

My next door neighbor was an alien. No, not an illegal immigrant, although I suppose he was in a manner of speaking. What I mean though is that he was not one us - that he came from another planet, or another dimension, or somewhere other. Oh, he looked human enough to pass. If you had run into him on the street, or in a bar, you'd never have thought there was anything amiss. Even though he lived right next door to me, I was completely fooled for a long time. I mean, he'd been there for most of a year before I even began to suspect the truth.

My neighbor always kept pretty much to himself. I did see him occasionally, of course. He cut the grass regularly and brought in his infrequent mail and if I waved or shouted a greeting, he waved back and even nodded recognition once or twice. Until I grew suspicious and began to watch more closely, I had never heard him speak. He went out on very rare occasions, always on foot – didn't own a car, but not often and he obviously didn't have a job. That was one of the first peculiarities I noticed, but I figured he was either independently wealthy or worked from home. He was not nearly old enough to be retired like me. Not once in the two years since he had moved in had he ever entertained a visitor that I knew of, and the one time I saw a pair of Jehovah's Witnesses ring his bell, they never made it past the threshold.

I should describe him. His name, according to the registrar of deeds and the name on the mailbox, was Peter Strange. I looked him up on the internet but found nothing of interest, just his name and address. He might have had a cell phone, but I couldn't track down a listing. He resembled a nondescript white male about six feet tall, moderate weight, no obvious distinguishing marks, a full head of slightly grey hair. I'd guess he would have been in his late forties, if he'd been human. There was nothing unusual about his appearance or the way he dressed – invariably shirts and jeans. He shoveled the snow off his front walk in the winter but never bothered with the driveway. There was no cable connection to his house.

A little peculiar, you say, but nothing to suggest he wasn't just a mildly eccentric human being. That's what I thought too.

At this point, you probably think I'm imagining things. I mean, what would an alien be doing living in a quiet neighborhood in a sleepy suburb of a mostly somnolent metropolis? Advance guard for an invasion force? Seems unlikely. Observing the human condition in preparation for contact? Not the best place for it, and with no television, no car, and few trips away from the house, he wouldn't be getting much observing done. Hiding from his enemies? He could breathe our air, eat our food, looked just like us, and knew enough to acquire money and buy a piece of property. But I've seen that movie and I knew that meant they'd find him sooner or later. If that was the case, I might end up being collateral damage in the explosive climax.

So what tipped me off? I suppose it started with the birdbath, although I didn't think much of it then. Strange had a postage stamp sized backyard. There was a flower garden where he carefully tended a plot of – are you ready for this? – dandelions and violets. Shortly after he moved in, his furniture all brand new and purchased at a single store. There was a smaller delivery which brought his mailbox, garden tools, and a birdbath. It was a perfectly ordinary birdbath and he placed it at the exact center of his tiny back yard, nothing unusual about that except that it stood there upside down. It was invisible from the street but I noticed it almost every time I was outside in the yard.

Okay, that wasn't much to hang a deep suspicion on, I grant you, and other than finding it rather odd I wouldn't have thought of it again. But it was just the first clue.

The first few times I saw him outside, I tried to start up a conversation. On each occasion, he smiled and nodded or waved, but immediately turned and went into the house. I was miffed at first, amused later, and after a while paid no more attention to him than if he'd been just another pesky squirrel trying to find a way into my attic. The first time we had a heavy snowfall, I got up early, drank a cup of coffee, swaddled myself in layers of clothing, and went outside to deal with the front walk. I noticed then that Strange had already shoveled a path to his mailbox and cleared the sidewalk to each end of his property. The path was precisely the same width from beginning to end, no sloppiness anywhere. I approved, but I figured he must have gotten up before the sun to get that much work done so quickly.

It only snowed twice more that winter, but Strange's pattern never altered. Not once did I see him shoveling. Not once did I hear him from my bedroom.

Then there was the garbage. Or rather, the lack of garbage. The town picks up on Thursdays and I dutifully trundled out my green bin for recycled paper, my blue bin for glass and metal, my grey plastic garbage pail, and occasionally trash bags full of assorted debris. I did occasionally see my neighbor carrying out his recycling bins, but he never had any garbage or miscellaneous trash. I noticed this fairly early in our non-relationship, but shrugged it off. As I became more curious, I started casually walking up the street so that I could sneak a look into his recycling bins. The bottles and cans were always spotlessly clean, their labels removed so I could not determine what their former contents had been. The only thing in the green bin was junk mail.

So maybe he has a garbage disposal, I told myself. Or he composts it to make his dandelions grow stronger. Still, it was another oddity.

Then there were the dogs. We have a couple in the neighborhood whose owners let them run loose. Neither of them are vicious, although the terrier barks a good fight, and other than occasionally having to clean up after them, I've never been inconvenienced. The other one, a mutt, came into my yard while I was trimming my hedge one day last summer, obviously looking for a good spot to take a dump. I glared at him and he took the hint, slipping through the hedge into my neighbor's yard. He was just assuming the proper position when the front door opened.

Strange's face remained perfectly neutral and he neither spoke nor gestured. He just stood there staring and the dog gave a little shake, then bolted for the street. It paused there for a second, gave one defiant bark, and ran off. I've never seen a dog on Strange's property since. No cats either. No squirrels for that matter. And there aren't any birds nesting in his trees or picking grubs out of his grass, not even the robins who follow me when I use the mower.

So toward the middle of the summer, I started to put all of these pieces together, except they wouldn't fit. Individually, they weren't worth much, but as a package, they suggested only that my neighbor's name had been well chosen. I started paying more attention.

I have already mentioned that Strange had no television. I manufactured excuses to work in the yard, mostly on his side of the house, and I never heard a sound from inside. Not even a slamming door, a chirping microwave, or a sneeze. I found a spot from which I could look in through his kitchen window without being obvious. The counters were bare and clean, cupboard doors neatly closed. There were no magnets or notes taped to the portion of the refrigerator that I could see, and I never noticed any pots or pans on the stove. Once or twice Strange was sitting or standing there, but he was always motionless and I always got bored and turned away before he moved.

I sent him flowers anonymously one day "from a shy friend", just to see what would happen. He accepted them from the delivery man and I was close enough to hear him speak for the very first time. There was only a single word. "Thanks." But I had a new bit of data. Strange sounded like a throat cancer victim fitted with a voice box. You know, one of those things that sound flat and mechanical, as though it was translating from an alien language. Exactly. That was the first time the possibility of his alien nature occurred to me, and I laughed at myself for being overly imaginative.

Once a year I spend a week on Block Island. It's a bit of an extravagance given the size of my pension, but I budget for it carefully and it's the only chance I have to travel since I retired from my job as security supervisor at Eblis Manufacturing - forty years spent watching grainy views of the perimeter fences. I gave up my own car a while back, just couldn't justify keeping it, so I always hire a cab to take me to the ferry and rent a moped while I am on the island. A few days before I was due to leave last year, I had a sudden inspiration. Why not ask Strange to keep an eye on the house for me? I wasn't really concerned that anyone would break in; I didn't have much of anything worth stealing. But it provided an excuse to engage him in a conversation.

So the next day I went over and rang his doorbell.

The door swung open so quickly that I realized he must have been standing right behind it. Probably he'd seen me coming up his front walk. His face wore its usual bland mask and he didn't speak.

"Hi, I'm Ed Gates, from next door. I don't mean to disturb you but I was wondering if you could do me a favor?"

No response, not even a blink. It was mildly unsettling.

I pretended not to have noticed and rushed on. "I'm going to be away next week and I was wondering if you'd keep an eye on the house while I'm gone. I've been having trouble with a couple of the neighborhood kids and I don't want them trashing the place." This wasn't entirely untrue. Two teenaged girls had sneaked into my heavily shaded back yard for an illicit smoke and I'd chased them out while they swore at me.

"I don't go out very often." I already knew about the voice box, but his reply was still startling.

"No problem. You don't have to actually do anything. Just, you know, call the police if you see anyone who shouldn't be there."

He seemed to be considering things. "I don't have a telephone."

Well, I'd sort of guessed that too, but I wasn't really looking for a house sitter. I had hoped to be invited inside so that I could get a good look around, but had to be content with what I could see through the open door. A couch, chairs, end tables, lamps, mirror on one wall. No paintings. Nothing at all on the built in shelves. Shag carpet on the floor.

"Well, if you just let them know you've seen them, they'll probably run away. I don't want to put you to any trouble."

He didn't reply, but of course, I hadn't asked a question. The silence hung between us like a spent teabag. "Thanks, then. Have a nice day."

The door closed, not quite in my face.

So now it was more than curiosity. It had become a challenge. For the first time, I didn't really enjoy my vacation on Block Island because I was impatient to get back and pursue my investigation. I sat on the broad porch of the Gothic Inn, drinking lemonade and plotting ways of finding out more about my enigmatic neighbor. I was standing on the dock waiting for the ferry when it came time to go home.

No, I didn't talk to anyone about what I suspected. What do you suppose your reaction would be if an elderly man living by himself should whisper to you that his next door neighbor wasn't a human being? I liked my little house. I didn't want to trade it for a shared room in a state run home for the demented. Before I could approach anyone else, I needed definitive proof although, to be honest, I was more interested in satisfying my own curiosity than alerting the world. The world at large had little interest in my welfare, and I reciprocated.

My first ploy was not very clever. I walked to the phone booth at the convenience store a block over and called in an anonymous complaint of a disturbance at 323 Dorrance Street. The Managansett police arrived before I made it back home. Two officers spoke briefly to Strange at the door, then went inside. I could hear the buzz of his voice box but couldn't make out any of the words. They were out of sight for a minute or two, then emerged, one turning to say something to Strange. He didn't respond and closed the door behind them.

Next I bought myself a video camera with a link to an external hard drive. I took this step with some misgivings because it meant I'd have to economize somewhere else, and there wasn't much fat in my budget. Maybe I would have to skip Block Island for a year. Maybe I'd be dead by then and it wouldn't matter.

I mounted the camera at an angle facing down from the window of my guest bedroom – which hasn't seen a guest in all the years I've lived here. There were a few branches in the way but I trimmed most of them back. This provided a panoramic view of Strange's front yard and most of the narrow strip of grass on the near side. I would have preferred to shoot through his front window, but the angles were wrong and he always kept the drapes closed anyway.

When he took out the garbage a few days later, I was ready at the window and immediately zoomed in, hoping to pick up some detail that might tell me something. He made two trips, one with each bin, setting them down precisely at the corner of his driveway. At the end he turned and, instead of returning to his house, he quite deliberately looked directly up at me. I flinched and backed away, feeling a surge of guilty panic, and when I returned to the window, he was gone.

I went over the recordings several times that afternoon. Until those last few seconds, everything had seemed quite ordinary. But there was no doubt in my mind that he had known that I was watching.

After my initial alarm died down, I felt paradoxically happy. Up until now I had been merely curious. Now it was a contest, a duel of wits between myself and this Strange character, person, whatever he was. For the first time in three years, I looked forward to rising in the morning. There was a purpose to my life. One way or another, I was going to outwit Mr. Strange and discover his secrets. I never doubted that I would eventually succeed.

But the next few weeks were discouraging. My surveillance netted me nothing but an occasional glance upward and once, I'm pretty sure, he winked at me, although it might have been just a bad spot in the recording. My enthusiasm began to wane and might have faded out if he hadn't issued a challenge of sorts.

The doorbell rang and I went to answer it. There was a delivery man standing on my doorstep with a vase full of flowers. I accepted it in some confusion and then he was gone and I was back inside fumbling open the small envelope pinned to one stem. "From a shy friend."

It occurred to me for the first time that I might be in personal danger. Although I had hunted a bit as a young man, I no longer owned a firearm of any sort. There were some serious knives in my kitchen, but I couldn't see myself waving a cleaver in Strange's face. Ultimately I decided that it didn't matter. If he was going to zap me with a death ray or impose his will on me through some version of telepathy or transform himself into a fanged monster with a ravenous appetite for human flesh, I wasn't going to be able to put up much of a fight even if I had bandoliers wrapped around my body and a Bowie knife clenched between my teeth.

So I decided to take a more civilized approach. "Hi, neighbor. I notice you're an alien and was wondering if you're here to slaughter me and everyone I know. Want to come to my place and talk about it over a drink?"

Well, maybe not quite that civilized. I was still trying to devise a strategy when events took matters out of my hands. About midnight one day in August, lightning hit Strange's house and started a fire.

He had managed to escape without injury, but it was obvious that the fire department was more interested in containing than extinguishing the blaze. I came outside in a bathrobe and slippers and joined the crowd that was watching Strange's house slowly collapse in upon itself. Perhaps ten minutes passed before it occurred to me to wonder about my neighbor. I found him standing near but not a part of the cluster of people to my left, staring at the crumbling, spitting, smoking ruins of his home with an expression of complete neutrality.

Despite my conviction that he was not a human being, I felt a surge of understandable sympathy and I insist that when I approached him, it was an act of consideration rather than an attempt to pursue my own agenda. "Would you like coffee or something, Mr. Strange?" He was wearing pale colored pajamas. "And I think we're about the same size if you want to borrow some clothes."

He looked at me, blinked once, his raspy voice expressing no emotion whatsoever. "Thank you. That could be useful."

I led him away.

Strange showed no curiosity about my house, followed me to the kitchen, and only took a seat at the narrow table when I repeated my invitation. I made a pot of coffee, thinking furiously because now that I had him on my turf, so to speak, I felt more confident. I poured a cup of steaming liquid and slid it across the table to him, then proffered the sugar bowl and a carton of skim milk.

He never looked up. The coffee went down in a single long gulp even though it was boiling hot. Then he drained the carton of milk, and ate all of the sugar out of the bowl, licking the inside clean. "Thank you. That was refreshing."

I had a cup of coffee in my hand as well, and even though I never took it black, I began to sip at it that way out of necessity. I sat down across from my neighbor and tried to think. Despite his strange behavior, I realized that he looked more human than I remembered. There was even a hint of expression in his face. His eyes spoke of sadness and his shoulders suggested resignation.

"Are you going to be all right?"

"My time has come at last." His voice sounded different somehow, less mechanical, and his face showed a hint of animation. His head turned and he looked around slowly, letting his eyes trail over my kitchen as though it was some alien exhibition to which he'd been admitted. "So many things. You won't need them now."

I didn't know how to respond to that and for the first time in a long while I wondered if maybe Strange wasn't an alien after all. Maybe he was just crazy.

He stood up slowly and smiled. It looked very much out of place on his face, but it was a smile. "You have been kind. May I shake your hand?"

It would have been churlish to refuse. His grip was firm but it felt funny. It was warmer than I expected and there was an odd texture to the skin. There was a kind of prickling sensation that went away almost immediately, and I would have wondered about it more at the time except that Peter Strange promptly dropped dead in the middle of my kitchen.

The paramedics were right outside but they couldn't do anything. "Must have been a stroke," one of them told me. "He was probably gone before he hit the floor."

The wreckage next door has been cleared away and there's a For Sale sign at the front end of the lot. I went to Strange's funeral. I was the only mourner. They must have performed an autopsy, but if they found anything extraordinary, they're keeping it under wraps.

A chapter of my life has just come to an end, but another has only begun. When I look around, I experience a kind of double vision, as though another set of eyes has been superimposed on mine. Or perhaps I have become a kind of organic camera and I somehow sense whoever, or whatever, is monitoring my input.

I no longer go out very often, even to shop. I have a standing order with the local grocer which is delivered to the house on Mondays. At mealtimes I become ravenously hungry. I no longer cook my food, nor is there any waste; I eat husks, seeds, fat, and peelings that I would previously have thrown into the garbage, then carefully wash the containers and remove the labels. I haven't seen a dog in my yard for weeks and the squirrels have stopped trying to get into my attic. Now that I'm paying my bills electronically, the only mail I receive is junk which I place immediately into the recycling bin. I had my cable television stopped because I am no longer interested. I did spend a few days rearranging things to make the house easier to maintain, throwing out box after box of stuff I have no use for. When I was done I realized that the night table in my bedroom was sitting upside down, but it doesn't seem worth the trouble to set it upright, particularly since I no longer sleep more than a few minutes per night. I mow the lawn carefully every Thursday. I have canceled the local newspaper.

This week I realized that I hadn't used the telephone for over a month and called to discontinue the service. When I spoke, I noticed that my voice is growing husky, metallic, and artificial. Today I'm going to replant the flower garden. Dandelions are quite pretty, don't you think? And they require so little care.

# KARMA SUTRA

The trouble started when someone invented a device that eavesdropped on the collective subconscious of the human race, although Paul Alford didn't make the connection until the night his dream was interrupted.

He had gone to bed early after returning from the holotheater where he'd thoroughly enjoyed Winona Bullock's scanty costuming in *Terminator 12*, and he was slipping into an unimaginative but satisfying wish fulfillment dream in which the beautiful time traveler rewarded him for his assistance by spending the night with him. She approached the bed, smiling broadly, and reached behind her back to unsnap the translucent halter top.

And froze in place.

A serious looking man in a retro haircut entered the room.

"Mr. Alford, are you aware of the fact that you are violating copyright?"

The dream Paul blinked and the real eye quivered in sympathy. "I have no idea what you're talking about."

"I am a recorded karma applet created by Norris Promotions, Inc. Under the Protection of Personal Resources provision of last year's Uniform Copyright Reform Act, you are prohibited from using the likeness of my client, to wit Winona Bullock, in any waking or sleeping dream unless you have previously paid the appropriate royalty."

"Royalty?"

"That's correct. We offer a wide variety of licenses, ranging from single night cameo appearances through unlimited use for pre-arranged periods of time. Ms Bullock offers participation up to and including several variations of conventional sex, although anything kinky is specifically prohibited."

"How much would it cost me for, umm, a one night stand. Simple sex, maybe a little bit of adventure in between sessions to keep things interesting."

The dream agent quoted a figure.

"No way. I could buy a copy of the holo for that."

"That is your prerogative. Our prices, however, are non-negotiable." He blinked out and, a moment later, so did the now inanimate actress.

Paul's subconscious was easily imprinted, and the following evening he studied a picture of Uma Pfeiffer before bedtime. His dreams that evening were entirely satisfactory, a situation that continued until the weekend, when a portly, redhaired man interrupted a dream to inform him that Ms Pfeiffer was now a client of his agency. By the end of the month, all of his favorite celebrities were off limits, and thirty days after that, he was having trouble finding bit players who hadn't signed up for Protection of Personal Resources.

Although it was less satisfactory, he was forced to resort to dreaming about people he actually knew, Dolores Cortiz down at the bank, Sarah Ames from the gymnasium, and when he was desperate for variation, Carla Scott, his slightly overweight neighbor. From time to time he was tempted to shell out the credit for a night with Goldie Streep or another of the less expensive stars, but his budget was tight at the best of times, and in any case he didn't like the idea of paying for sex, even dream sex.

On the first day of summer, Paul had just set the scene for a romantic interlude with Sarah Ames when a short haired woman with a stern expression materialized in the middle of the prison camp where he was planning an elaborate rescue. "I am here to inform you that my client, Sarah Janes Ames, has registered under the Protection of Personal Resources clause, which precludes use of her likeness without prior written permission."

Dolores Cortiz and even Carla Scott had signed on within the month.

Paul's subconscious tried to improvise for the next several weeks, creating imaginary women out of bits and pieces of memory. Sometimes it worked, but more often his creations would slowly assume the attributes of a single real person, at which point the automatic dream agent would appear, often interrupting at the most inauspicious moment.

Paul had nearly reached the point where he dreaded sleep and the frustrations that would accompany his dreaming when the pirate appeared.

He had just aborted a pretty good wish fulfillment sequence in which he rescued an almost recognizable Jennifer Michelle Holmes from a squad of stock Nazi stormtroopers when her dream agent appeared and advised him he was infringing on copyright by dreaming of too close an approximation. Paul was standing in a slowly fading war torn French countryside, waiting for the dream to fade completely, when an anachronistic pirate, complete with parrot, pegleg, and patch, stepped out from behind a tree.

"Hey, mate. I think I can help you." He winked the one good eye lasciviously.

"Not in your dreams," Paul responded. "And definitely not in mine."

"No, you don't understand me. I mean, I can fix you up with the woman you want."

"Yeah, I've seen the rate schedules. Too rich for my budget."

"There's ways around the rules, mate. You see, when you pay for a license, they let you draw this packet of karma. The karma travels through the collective subconscious. But what they don't want you to know is, there's ways to record a copy of those packets if you have the right equipment. Now I won't lie to you. The copies aren't quite as good as the original. Sometimes the hair color is wrong, or the voice is a little funny, or some other detail gets lost or messed up. But we charge ten percent what the big agencies do, and you only pay once. We tag the packet to your personal subconscious node, and you can draw on it as many times as you want."

Paul thought about it. "I don't know. Isn't this illegal or something?"

"Technically, but why should all these hotshot celebrities and their agents make money because of your dreams? After all, you're doing all the work. You're the creative one. Look, I'll give you our account number. Remember it tomorrow. Think about it and give us a call."

And he did, for almost an hour, then made the call, transferred the credit, and purchased an unregistered karma copy of his first love, Winona Bullock.

That night, Paul could hardly wait to fall asleep. He had done everything he possibly could while conscious to predispose himself to the dream he wanted, and sure enough, he found himself in a lovely southern mansion with his enthusiastic new wife. After some

74

hasty preliminaries, they retired to the bedroom, where she slowly began to disrobe. And sneezed. And sneezed again.

Naked at last, she joined him in bed, her nose bright red and running, eyes watering, and the other symptoms of a bad cold becoming so irritating that at last he rolled away from her in frustration.

It figures, he thought before drifting off into deeper, dreamless sleep. Buy a bootleg copy from a pirate, and you're almost certain to end up with a virus.

# SHADOW AND SUBSTANCE

Sonia Kester's parties were always crowd scenes, even when few people actually attended.

I threaded my way through the press of real and simulated bodies from the ballroom to the patio, drawing in a deep breath of the relatively cool night air. The deformed second of Inspiration's four moons crawled through the night sky, its irregular perimeter shivering animatedly as the image passed through the humid atmosphere.

"Driven out by the crowd, Sean?"

I turned and spotted Chari Kourie standing in a shadowed corner, walked slowly in her direction. "I prefer to think of it as voluntary exile, actually."

There were a half dozen real people scattered across the slagstone patio; it was an unwritten house rule that projecting guests remain indoors where the light was better, and Sonia's resident AI system could not port the images it generated beyond the walls of her sprawling home.

"Doesn't that amount to the same thing?"

I shrugged. "I'm just not the gregarious type. What's your excuse?"

Chari's eyes betrayed uneasiness. "I prefer to spend my time with real people."

"Don't they use projection on Tedium?" Chari had originally come to Inspiration on vacation, but had fallen in love with our picturesque seacoasts, rugged mountain chains, and spectacular cave systems. She had applied for extended residence, and was currently on the waiting list for full citizenship. Although we knew each other reasonably well, she rarely spoke of her home world except to describe it as drab and provincial, aptly named by its original settlers.

An autobar wandered in our direction and she delayed her answer until it had served us fresh drinks.

"Some of the big corporations use it, for meetings and inspection tours, but not for anything as trivial as this." She gestured vaguely back into the ballroom. "There's not a whole lot of money on Tedium; no resources to develop, although they have managed to become self sufficient. Not like here."

Inspiration depended heavily on the tourist trade. Some of the native lifeforms were in fact edible, but they provided little nourishment for our metabolisms. Vitamin supplements were manufactured locally, but we were still dependent on imports for a large portion of our food, despite relatively successful efforts at introducing bioengineered plants.

"Better get used to them," I ventured. "They're the wave of the future."

"Oh, it's not the projections that bother me. It's those others."

She obviously meant the AI's, Sonia's specialty. Sonia Kester had become a very wealthy woman after leaving the government research laboratories on Endeavor to form her own company. There had been considerable litigation, the government contending that she used knowledge and techniques she'd developed while in their employ in order to establish the first commercial AI distributorship in the region. Sonia was a ruthless and determined woman, however; she fought against every restriction they sought to impose, winning in some cases, ignoring or subverting rulings that went the other way. And she'd become very successful on her own; her obsessive attention to detail had become almost a trademark, although some of her critics accused her of intellectual exhibitionism.

"How can you tell the difference?"

"I sometimes can't. That's part of the problem." She'd been sipping tentatively, now drank more deeply. "They're creepy."

"Oh, I don't see that. It's a logical extension of the technology. Unless you retreat to some primitive world, you're going to run into more and more applications. And if you pay attention, you can always tell the real from the illusory."

Chari made an exasperated sound. "Don't patronize me, Sean. I'm not talking about AI'd restaurants or vehicles. I don't mind dealing with computers, even computers that are smarter than I am. I just don't like it when they look human. It doesn't feel right."

I almost chided her for believing in bogeymen but her voice was so laden with emotion, I decided to back off. Chari and I were not exactly friends, but we weren't unfriends either, and she was one of the more attractive of the available women my age in this part of the continent. And she did seem to be in some genuine distress.

We were interrupted at that point by the arrival of Sonia herself, impressively gowned in a transmorphic fabric whose patterns and colors changed as she moved from one environment to another, always seeking the most flattering contrasts. Her hair was done up in an elaborately sculptured style, designed to resemble a fairy castle. Sonia was a birdlike woman, narrow bones, her flesh a clinging sheath of tissue drawn taut, but her fingers wrapped tightly around my upper arm as she joined us.

"Sean, I've been looking all over for you."

"Just stepped outside to enjoy your garden." I nodded toward the elaborate expanse of topiaries, interspersed with banks of flowering plants. "The tandillae smell wonderful."

"I wouldn't know," she tapped the side of her nose with one slender forefinger. "No sense of smell. Atrophy of the olfactory nerve in my childhood. Look, there's someone here tonight whom you just have to meet." She glanced toward Chari. "You too, my dear. Come along if you'd like."

There was a momentary hesitation, but Chari nodded and even managed a cheery smile. Or a good counterfeit.

"It was pure luck that I found out he was vacationing nearby. If I hadn't already scheduled this party, it would have been sufficient excuse for one."

We re-entered the main ballroom, a ridiculous extravagance for a woman who lived alone. Or at least, without any human companions. The main room was a hundred meters square, but at the north and south ends, a series of arches led through a maze of smaller rooms, many of which were occupied by clusters of people interested in more private conversations. There were at least two hundred guests in the ballroom proper, although I had no idea how many of them were actually present. The constant murmur of their conversations drowned out the background music, while discrete autobars moved quietly about their business.     "Now where did he go?" Sonia's question was not rhetorical. I could tell by the inclination of her head that she had directed the query through an implant to the house computer and was waiting for a reply. It came almost instantly. She now held Chari's arm as well as my own, and turned us toward the right.

We were approaching a cadaverously tall man standing with a slender woman under a crenellated arch when we were approached by Linden Roth, Sonia's business partner, a rude and compulsively argumentative man but an apparent genius at organization and finance. Rumor had it that he'd clandestinely acquired enough stock to exert significant pressure on Sonia, theoretically his employer.

"Sonia, we need to talk." He didn't so much as glance at Chari or I and his tone clearly demanded an immediate acquiescence. An autobar rolled up and looked inquiring at Sonia, Chari, and I, then rolled off when none of us placed an order.

"I told you already, Linden, that this is neither the time nor the place." Roth opened his mouth, then closed it abruptly. "I'll be in the Orchid Room, waiting for you, Sonia. We have to resolve this now, understand?" And he turned abruptly away, brushed past the two people in the arch without so much as acknowledging their existence, and was gone.

The cadaverous man was apparently our quarry, as he had already started in our direction. His companion was a spectacularly attractive young woman wearing a stylish sarong.

"Ser Dyle, I'd like you to meet two of my dearest friends." That was hardly the case, but neither of us was in a position to argue. "Sean Folle, Chari Kourie, this is Sandor Dyle."

I recognized the name immediately and extended my hand. "It's a pleasure to meet you, Ser Dyle. I've read several of your articles on probability plotting and pattern recognition. And naturally I've heard about your adventures on Copernicus and Thibault."

Dyle appeared vaguely uncomfortable as he shook hands with us both. "Just Sandor, please. I've never been at ease with formality. And the reports of my involvement in both those situations were grossly exaggerated. I simply applied the principles of my research to realtime situations in an advisory capacity. The Copernican authorities were already well along the way to capturing the Starport Strangler and the most that can be said is that I eliminated a few blind alleys."

"But the Thibault case," I protested mildly. "It's my understanding that you averted a full scale religious war by discovering the location of the stolen relics."

Dyle appeared to be genuinely uncomfortable. "The thieves were careless. I simply checked recordings of pedestrian traffic near the mosque against a model of changes in credit expenditure patterns. It was a lucky guess, but still essentially a guess. If the

Thibeau were not so adamant about avoiding even the most rudimentary law enforcement authority, the theft would have been solved without my help." He turned to our hostess. "Is this the promising young man you were telling me about?"

"The very one. Sean's a chaoticist; he thinks that no matter how elaborate our programming, we can't possibly anticipate real life, and all of our creations are inherently and inevitably flawed. I suppose you could say he has a view of the universe completely opposite your own." Sonia had released my arm and shifted her position to effectively block Chari out of the conversation, a movement which appeared casual but almost certainly was not. Neither had she bothered to introduce us to Dyle's companion.

"Not at all," Dyle demurred. "Pattern analysis simply implies that all activity, natural or human, creates a discernible profile given a sophisticated enough analysis. There are always data points that fall outside that profile. Pattern analysis is descriptive, not proscriptive."

Sonia's eyes betrayed her lack of interest, and she took advantage of a pause to extricate herself. "Well, I'll leave you two to talk shop, if you'll excuse me." Dyle and I both nodded.

"May I introduce Tarisha Chan." Dyle turned his body to include all three of us in his field of vision, and I raised my hand to grasp hers, even as the name registered. The tingle and tenuous resistance could have indicated she was projecting in from some other location, but the name told me she was an AI. Tarisha Chan was a famous hologram star whose career had been enhanced by a series of affairs with prominent individuals of both sexes. She had died nearly two centuries before I was born.

"A pleasure to meet you after all these years," I said ironically as I withdrew my hand from the weak but palpable field of force that surrounded projected images. Vibration of the membrane generated sounds, voices for example, and enabled projectees and AI's to communicate. But the field also helped establish a physical presence. If you bumped into a projection in a crowd, you knew immediately. I once lost my balance and fell directly through one of Sonia's "guests"; the experience was unsettling but not dangerous. Her lack of reality was underlined when the ubiquitous autobar rolled up and ignored her presence while offering itself to the rest of us; autobars were programmed to avoid AI's and projectees, of course.

Chari's discomfort was quite evident, and the AI picked it up right away. "If you'll excuse me," she said brightly, "Sonia made me promise to speak to Counsellor Ngambi, and he seems to be free at the moment."

"Certainly, my dear. We'll talk again later." Dyle must have known that she wasn't real, but he watched her disappear into the crowd with a faint hint of regret.

"Will you be staying on Inspiration for long?"

Dyle turned to Chari and his expression brightened again as he answered her question. "Alas, the <u>Demiurge</u> has a firm departure date only a few days from now. I shall only have a brief time to sample your world's scenery. I understand the southern continent has some quite spectacular chasms and underground rivers."

She nodded enthusiastically. "I've rafted down some of them. It's an unforgettable experience."

"A bit too adventurous for my blood, I'm afraid, though I would like to go on one of the more sedentary tours."

The three of us stood together for quite a long while. Dyle was a fascinating conversationalist. Not only did he reveal himself to be a witty repository of interesting anecdotes, but he made a quite deliberate effort to give Chari and I equal time and he listened to both of us with genuine or convincingly feigned interest. He remained unwilling to talk about his exploits as a detective, but proved to be knowledgeable in a number of other areas and the three of us chatted as though we'd known each other for years.

We were eventually interrupted by the arrival of Karis, whom Chari and I both knew to be one of Sonia's AI creations. She had done all of the design and much of the programming herself; it was as much a hobby as a business to her, and she prided herself on the verisimilitude of her constructs.

"Excuse me, please, but Ser Kester asks if you would mind rescuing her from a rather unpleasant conversation in the orchid room?"

I glanced at my companions. "I guess we could polish off our armor. Lead the way, Karis."

"That's all right," Chari interposed, speaking to the AI. "I know which is the orchid room."

Karis nodded and withdrew into the crowd.

Chari led us through a series of arches and open courts until we were far enough removed from the main room that the crowd had thinned appreciably. We had not yet reached our hostess when we heard her voice, high pitched and angry.

"For the last time, Linden, I've made my decision! If you're not happy with it, you're free to resign your position at any time!"

The unmistakable gravelly voice of Linden Roth replied in uncharacteristically emotional tones. "You're jeopardizing the entire fiscal structure of the company! I've spent years developing that financial base and I won't allow you to destroy it!"

Chari hesitated and glanced in my direction. I was even less willing to thrust myself into this situation than she; I worked for Sonia, but Roth approved all promotions and salary increases. No matter which of them I offended, it would work against my best interest.

"Perhaps I should go first," volunteered Dyle, correctly interpreting my reluctance.

Chari and I followed, entering the Orchid Room just as Roth exploded again. "You overestimate your influence, Sonia! My contract gives me final approval over all financial matters for so long as I'm employed, and I won't approve your proposal!"

They stood at the far end of the room, Sonia with her hands on her hips, Roth waving a nearly full glass of wine to illustrate his point. Sonia was rigid with anger, but when she answered, her voice was lower and back under control. "Very well, Linden. If that's the way it has to be, then your employment contract is terminated immediately. I am registering this decision via datalink as we speak. There's nothing you can do to stop the expansion now."

The three of us paused as Roth took a half step back, his face suddenly pale, shoulders slumping. The tableau held for a beat or two before his face suddenly twisted into an expression of such intense rage that I felt physically repelled.

"I won't let you do this to me, Sonia." Roth's hand slipped inside his shirt, and when it emerged, I blinked in confusion before recognizing what he held. The small, thin weapon was a Blossom, its possession illegal virtually everywhere. Blossoms fired a bioengineered dart that released into the bloodstream one of the less pleasant sidelights of nanotechnology, tiny destroyers who attacked the body's integrity from within. Even the slightest wound was invariably fatal. An ugly and undignified way to die.

Perhaps foolishly, Dyle and I both started forward, but Sonia was not quite as vulnerable as her small stature might suggest. A great deal happened in the next few seconds, but for me they seemed to pass in slow motion, every detail distinctly defined. She lunged forward, grappling with Roth, who raised his arms defensively, apparently surprised by her reaction. The wine glass fell to the carpet, bounced once and rolled toward the far end of the room. Their bodies pressed together, Sonia and Roth struggled for only a single beat before the faint whine of the Blossom, familiar to me from scores of holoshows, told us the weapon had been discharged.

But it was Linden Roth who fell to the floor, his mouth opening and closing in shock as he stared at the ceiling, a growing red stain in the center of his chest.

Dyle halted immediately, but my momentum carried me forward. I had almost reached them when Sonia turned, the Blossom still clutched in one hand, and waved me back. "Stay there! I've already called the LSU." Indeed, even as she spoke, a Life Support Unit rolled through the far door, stopped beside the body, extruded scores of febrile tentacles which wrapped the slumped form, then gently pulled Linden Roth's now motionless body into the waiting receptacle. With a faint mechanical sound, the LSU disappeared back the way it had come.

Sonia was visibly shaken, but her voice was calm and resolute as she handed the Blossom to Dyle.

"You'd better take this, Ser Dyle. I've also called the Enforcement Authority. They'll want it as evidence." Other guests were arriving now, a rising murmur to our rear. One, a man I'd never seen before, walked past us and picked up Roth's discarded glass. I started toward him, intending to recommend he not interfere with what was undoubtedly a crime scene, but Dyle caught hold of my arm.

"It doesn't matter," he said quietly. I frowned a question but he shook his head. "I'll explain later."

"It wasn't your fault," Chari was saying. "We all saw him threaten you."

Sonia nodded, just barely. "I realize that. But it's still rather a shock." She took a step, staggered slightly. "My dear, would you mind helping me to my room. I'm afraid my legs are a bit unsteady."

As Chari and our hostess disappeared through the archway, I turned to Dyle. Several of the other guests were milling about, speaking in hushed tones. "Do you think there's any chance they'll be able to bring him back?"

"None at all. The LSU was a wasted effort. No one has ever survived a Blossom." His expression was troubled and he was staring toward the spot where Roth had died. He was certainly correct; the LSU chamber would preserve Roth's body in its present state almost indefinitely, but it was a hopeless cause.

Dyle moved forward, crouched, his eyes sweeping the floor. "That's very interesting," he murmured softly.

"What is it, Sandor?"

He stood erect, wrinkled his nose. "Do you smell anything odd?"

I didn't understand what he was talking about, but obediently I sniffed the air. "No. Should I?"

Dyle didn't answer because we were interrupted at that moment by the arrival of a team of Enforcers, their official sashes a crimson slash across the white uniforms. They herded us into the ballroom, where we were all required to identify ourselves. Sonia had turned off all of the AI's, of course, and most of the projectees had terminated their presence as well, although technically speaking they were illegally absenting their viewpoints from the scene of a crime. The ballroom was considerably less crowded when the officials escorted an LSU out the front door, presumably bearing the body of Linden Roth.

Dyle and I were still together as we waited to give our statements.

"I hope this horrible accident won't ruin your visit to our world, Ser Dyle."

"I'd hardly call it an accident. Linden Roth was murdered."

I suppose I must have gaped because his eyes twinkled with amusement even though his expression was otherwise serious.

"I don't suppose you'd care to explain that?"

"In due course, if necessary. But with your training, you ought to be able to figure it out for yourself. Didn't you say earlier that you enjoyed logical puzzles?"

Our conversation was interrupted at that point by the officer in charge, a woman named Cumberly, who told us curtly that while they would proceed as quickly as possible, it would be necessary for those of us physically present to remain until each of us had been interviewed about the tragedy. Projectees were to provide their names and residence codes before disconnecting.

"How long do you suppose we'll be stuck here?"

Dyle shrugged. "Long enough to discover the truth of the matter."

I was thinking furiously. Obviously Dyle had seen something which I had missed.

"I don't suppose you'd give me a hint?"

"Giving up so easily? You might start by noticing who is missing from among our number." He gestured toward the milling crowd, now reduced to approximately four dozen, including ourselves.

It was a fruitless task. I didn't know all of those Sonia had invited, many had been projectees or AI's in any case. I said as much to Dyle. "Except for Sonia and Chari, of course, I have no way of knowing who was physically present in the first place who isn't here now."

"How do you know that I'm physically here, that I'm not a projection?"

"I can reach out and touch you." I did so, brushing his arm.

"And what if you were denied tactile proof? If you were in a room with an individual you could not touch, wouldn't you be able to tell the difference?"

"Yes, I suppose so. If I were watching for signs."

"And what signs would those be?"

"Shadows, incidental sounds like footsteps, the sound of breathing."

"Surely those could all be included in the programming?"

"Yes, but it's rarely done. There's no reason to mimic life in such detail."

"Well then, what if you were watching a hologram recording? Could you still determine who was real and who wasn't?"

"Possibly. It depends on what the recording showed. Sometimes you can pick up clues from how a projection interacts with the environment. One of our local politicians gave a speech by projection a few weeks back, and a brisk wind kept blowing leaves and other debris through his image."

Dyle nodded. "Then I ask you again, who is missing from our number?"

I thought about it, thought furiously, but still couldn't think of anyone. Dyle relented a bit.

"Let's try a different approach. How do they differentiate between the two?" He gestured toward one of the autobars, which had reverted to standby mode, accepting but not soliciting orders for fresh drinks.

"I don't actually know, now that you mention it. I assume they can detect the resonance of the projection field. They avoid passing through the images, but they don't offer to serve them."

"Precisely."

Something stirred in my memory, but I couldn't pin it down.

"Roth was holding a drink during the confrontation, was he not?"

"Yes, of course." The image of the empty glass rolling across the carpet was indelibly imprinted in my memory.

"But he didn't take a drink from the autobar when it approached you a few moments before, did he?"

I shrugged. "So he got one later. What does that..." I paused, realizing what Dyle was implying. "But we saw someone pick up the glass afterward," I protested.

"Did we? Could you point that gentleperson out to me now?"

I looked around the room, but the man was not among our number.

"They were projectees? Roth and the other man?"

"Not projectees, AI's. Linden Roth is dead, murdered by Sonia Kester, perhaps in the fashion we just witnessed, so to speak, but probably in cold blood and under circumstances less flattering to Ser Kester."

I shook my head. "But we saw the LSU pick up Roth's body." Dyle opened his mouth, but I answered myself before he could speak. "Another projection, of course."

"That's right. Roth's body was already in stasis in a real unit, undoubtedly dead of a Blossom wound to the chest, but I doubt very much that it was inflicted in the manner we were supposed to believe real."

"What made you suspect the truth?"

"I was suspicious right from the outset. The little melodrama was a bit too theatrical to be true; as a chaoticist, you should have suspected how neatly we were set up, first as witnesses to the early quarrel, then arriving precise in time for the final act, but not quickly enough to intervene. And then there was the odor, or rather the lack of one."

"Odor?" I remembered Dyle's query about whether or not I smelled anything.

"The smell of blood is unmistakable. I've had more than one exposure to it, so I perhaps had a slight advantage over you." His expression was briefly pained, but his features smoothed themselves out. "Those two observations led me to reconsider our earlier encounter and I remembered that just before we met, you were all served drinks by an autobar."

Something else fell into place. "The autobar didn't offer anything to Roth, so he really wasn't there. And Sonia has no sense of smell. It might never occur to her to program in olfactory stimuli."

My companion nodded. "You might also have noticed that although the phantom Roth dropped a nearly full wine glass in the struggle, there were no damp spots or stains on the white carpeting. He wasn't really there and neither was the drink."

I was convinced. "You'll have to tell them, Sandor. You can't let her get away with this."

For the first time since I'd met him, Dyle looked distinctly discomfited. "If you don't mind, Sean, I'd rather prefer that you advise Ser Cumberly of our observations. I'm here on vacation, and if my involvement were to be known," he sighed, "I'd spend the rest of my visit dodging the public and the media reporters."

I argued a bit but ultimately agreed to accede to Sandor's wishes. Truthfully, I wasn't averse to a little public recognition myself. With the death of one of the principle owners of the company that employed me, and the probable imprisonment of the other, I'd obviously be seeking new employment fairly soon. A little publicity couldn't hurt.

"I feel guilty about taking credit for this, but I'll do as you wish, Sandor. I confess that I'm frankly in awe of your powers of observation, though. To have noticed so many details, before there was even reason to do so, you must have a near photographic memory."

He coughed, glanced away, and his features were flushed with...could it be embarrassment?

"Actually, I might have been just as fooled as the rest of you if I wasn't so clumsy. Your gravity is a bit lighter than I am used to and when Ser Kester brought you to me, I stumbled a bit. My hand brushed against Ser Roth, or the illusion of Ser Roth, and I knew right from the outset that he wasn't really there. Constructing retroactive proof was child's play." He grinned childishly. "I told you my reputation was greatly exaggerated."

# INSIDE THE SPHERE

I never expected the project to succeed. I can admit that now, since the damage has already been done. Most of my colleagues probably felt the same way, but they're too busy congratulating themselves now for what was, essentially, nothing more than a stroke of luck to acknowledge that fact.

What kind of luck it was has yet to be determined, but I have my suspicions.

It was Teresa Garfield, or her team anyway, who made the actual breakthrough. My first hint of what was to come consisted of a knock on my office door just as I was about to call it a day.

"Come in."

The words were unnecessary. Teresa had opened the door and entered my office a fraction of a second after knocking. The woman had no sense of privacy or personal space, although admittedly she tolerated intrusions into her own areas that would have set my teeth on edge. As usual, her clothing clashed violently; she favored bright, even garish colors, but apparently used random selection while dressing.

"Nelly, you have to come down to the womb."

The "womb" was our experimental chamber, so named because of a coincidental similarity in shape, christened by Teresa herself, the day she arrived at the project.

"What now, Teresa? Another meltdown?" Hyperbole was our defense mechanism, a shield against the cumulative effects of having to experience one failed experiment after another.

We were engaged in some pretty arcane research, funded by the government for reasons of its own. Roger Powell, our Project Director, derived a strange sort of satisfaction from the fact that after six full years of work, we had yet to produce a single useful result, not even a promising spinoff. Considering the state of the economy and the mindset of the current administration, it's surprising we've retained our funding. I can only attribute our longevity to a comparatively modest budget and an immodest amount of bureaucracy.

The project mandate was vague enough that several of us were openly using the Center's resources to pursue our own interests under the guise of collateral relevance. These intellectual excursions were always justified as contributing to our overall mission, but some of those Statements of Justification were so tenuous that even a lay person might have detected lapses of logic.

"No, nothing like that. We seem to have made a breakthrough."

I raised my eyebrows. As I said, none of us really believed there was any chance of succeeding.

I haven't mentioned the subject of our work, have I? Project Sesame was created to investigate certain peculiar aspects of spatial distortion observed after the Southwest Supercollider first became operational and before its unfortunate destruction by terrorists. Using a variety of resources, we were attempting to recreate the phenomenon, independent of the supercollider itself. Our mission statement urged us to investigate "the possibility that there exists a means of abrogating some of the constraints imposed by the Einsteinian view of the universe through distortion of the underlying fabric of the physical universe."

In other words, we were supposed to determine whether or not it was possible to punch a hole through space and find a shortcut to other worlds.

There was evidence that the phenomenon had been revealed rather than created by the particle accelerator. We had been divided into three teams, each with its own chosen avenue of approach. Teresa Garfield, a brilliant if somewhat unconventional physicist, was investigating the relationship of time and space, to determine whether it was possible to separate the two artificially. Oliver Dembo was a mathematician and sometimes poet, his team engaged in a purely abstract analysis of the phenomenon. Director Powell was exploring the possibility that the mysterious distortion had been a reflection not of another point in our universe, but another plane of existence entirely. Although Roger was nominally Project Director, he rarely left his laboratory and was acutely uncomfortable when asked to make a decision.

As for me, I, Dr. Nelson Lynch, was the official debunker. Oh, that wasn't the title in my personnel file. My job description was "Interdisciplinary Coordinator" and I was supposed to keep each group of investigators apprised of the work being performed elsewhere, to avoid duplication of effort and to stimulate the separate strains through interfertilization. My transfer to Sesame was categorized as a lateral reassignment, but when one's marriage to the daughter of the National Council of Scientific Development ends messily, one accepts punishment as gracefully as possible.

I actually spent most of my time mediating conflicting requests for use of our limited computer time and writing summaries of failed experiments that no one bothered to read. It was a wasteful, often frustrating position, but it left me free to pursue my own research, which involved certain anomalies in energy transformations.

"Another breakthrough?" I was less than enthused. "It seems to me that the last time you had a breakthrough, it was a miscalibration. And the time before that, the results were irreproducible and probably caused by a fault in the interruptible power source."

She nodded wearily. "I know. And the time before that it was a malfunctioning chipset. But this time I'm sure we've found a genuine misalignment between the continua. You have to come see."

I really didn't want to. My work is no longer the most important part of my life. Sandy Michalski had invited me for dinner at her apartment, and the atmosphere between the two of us had been growing steadily warmer for weeks. She was the first woman I'd felt comfortable with since my divorce two years earlier.

"Teresa, I have plans for this evening. Major plans."

"Cancel them. When you see what I have to show you, you'll be ready to stay through the night."

I didn't believe her, but she was right.

To be honest I'd never really been convinced that the original observations had been accurate. Oh, something unusual happened in Texas all right; the evidence was too data rich and mutually collaborative to dismiss. There'd been some kind of alteration of the inter-relationship of matter inside the operational area, perhaps even a violation of what the public called the law of gravity. But the space time continuum could not have been ruptured, as had been claimed by certain sensationalist popularizers.

"One second the chamber was empty and the next..." Teresa waited while I examined her prize.

There was a tiny field of distortion centered in the Aspect Chamber. Even with the enhancement available, it resembled a poorly rendered hologram, perfectly spherical, suspended in space.

"Not much to look at." My comment was dry but I was already excited. I'm not a technician, but I understood enough to interpret the readings displayed on the monitor. I didn't know what Teresa had stumbled onto, but it was certainly interesting. There was the faintest suggestion of a solid form within the sphere, too indistinct to identify.

"Can you sharpen the image any?"

She shook her head. "Magnification just makes it worse. We're going to do a full 360 degree survey, with topological mapping. It's queued up for processing later tonight."

"Queued up? What's ahead of it?"

"Oliver's latest extrapolation. Estimated processing time four hours."

"Did Roger approve that? It's an outrageous drain on our computer resources."

She nodded. "It's been on the task management docket for almost a week. Roger gave it 'as available' priority and no one else had anything scheduled for this evening, so it went into the active queue."

"But Oliver isn't even here!" He'd left the day before to attend a weeklong conference in Minsk, with a little side trip to a ski resort in Switzerland. "Can't you get Roger to approve an override?"

"Gone for the day. In transit. And he still refuses to carry a cell phone. By the time he gets home, the program will be running, and an abort requires approval from the requesting party."

"Then we'll just have to wait." And we did. Sandy did not sound happy when I called.

The results of the mapping, which were not available until well after midnight, were tantalizing and frustrating. Stripped of the technical terms, what we learned was that our visual observations were confirmed; there was some kind of distortion of space. But the analysis of the actual appearance of the distortion was, well, weird.

"Every run through has different results on a point by point basis." Teresa sounded puzzled.

"That's not surprising. There must be some kind of fluctuation that's too rapid for us to detect visually."

She shook her head. "You don't understand. I expected at least some variation from one time slice to another. But when I run the same data through the visual enhancement subroutine, I get a different profile."

"A distortion in the recording tape?"

"No. I'm using the same source file. It's interpreting the exact same data differently every time I run it."

That made no sense. She was effectively telling me that the computer was adding the same column of figures over and over, getting a different sum each time, and all of them valid.

"There's got to be a programming or system error. Did you check the Monitor function?" The Monitor was a memory resident safeguard that constantly checked running programs to ensure their integrity.

"Errorlevel is zero."

"Then the Monitor itself is malfunctioning."

"I don't think so."

Roger was less than happy to find us waiting for him in the morning.

"Okay, I guess it's worth investigating further. I'll give you priority on the computers for the next forty-eight hours. And I'll call Oliver and tell him to get his ass back here. He can ski any time."

My own work was stalled anyway, so I joined Teresa in her lab, telling myself not to get excited just yet. One promising observation after another had proven itself barren, and I had never been good about accepting disappointments.

Late that afternoon, one of the technicians inadvertently cut power to the wrong module and shut down the field.

"Let's pay more attention, people." Teresa didn't raise her voice, but the undertone was warning enough. "Prepare for field regeneration."

I was expecting nothing to happen this time, but the sphere returned, although this time the interior was different.

"Is that a tree?" I stepped to the safety rail, squinting to bring the shape into focus.

"Looks like a feather," observed one technician.

"Or a serrated knifeblade," Teresa said thoughtfully. Other opinions ranged from a skeletal arm to the snout of a cannon.

"What about surface integrity?" Roger had joined us in the Womb, and we all crowded around the Aspect Chamber.

"Preliminary tests show a measurable pseudoviscous pressure, but we haven't as yet attempted a breach." Teresa shook her head. "It's like an oversized, underinflated beach ball."

"Would that be wise?" Truthfully, I was a bit nervous about probing too quickly. We still had no idea what we were dealing with.

"It's the logical next step," Teresa answered. "We have a controlled environment within the Aspect Chamber, there are safeguards to cut the power within a millisecond if certain parameters are exceeded. There's some risk, of course, but that's true with any groundbreaking experiment."

We both turned to Roger. It was up to him, of course, as Project Director. He licked his lips and turned away, studying the cracks in the cement wall on the opposite side of the Womb.

"Assuming that proper safeguards are in place and have been personally audited by the presiding team leader," he said finally, "I see no reason not to proceed in a systematic fashion."

Or, in plain English, go ahead, Teresa, since you're going to take the fall if anything goes wrong.

Nothing did. Not at first anyway. Microfilamentary probes were extruded until they reached the surface of the sphere. Some additional energy was required to actually break the meniscus, but no more than you might expect piercing a soap bubble. We were all holding our breath at the time, imagining spectacular explosions or implosions, a rent in the fabric of space and time, some unimaginable and indescribable catastrophe.

The reality was actually rather dull.

The first penetration was for a duration of precisely one millisecond. There was no discernible effect on the portion of the probe which had crossed the barrier. Subsequent tests at regular intervals yielded the same results. By the end of the week, we were ready to insert a camera in the head of our probe.

The results this time were more bizarre than ever.

"There's no measurable improvement in the clarity of the recorded images," Teresa observed. "And there's something else..." She let the sentence hang.

"Do I whistle a trumpet fanfare of murmur an ominous drumroll?" The jest covered a flash of annoyance; I don't like being manipulated. But Teresa never noticed the sarcasm.

"There's a peculiar inconsistency. Our secondary recordings of the original photographs and tapes are still absolutely vivid, but the originals of these and our subsequent tapings vary with each viewing."

That's what she said, and later demonstrated. The images from flat tape and holographs were different every time we ran them through the console. Not radically so, but colors and other details were in a constant state of flux.

Oliver, back from abroad, had an unnerving suggestion. "It's as though the original is only a template, a model from which the copies were extrapolated. I wonder if what we're seeing here is a bonafide abstraction, and every attempt we make to interpret the phenomenon in absolute terms is at best an approximation."

Teresa suggested that we enlist some schizophrenics to view the films, but Roger overruled the proposal as scientifically unverifiable.

"We've kept our funding because we're invisible. Let someone in Congress hear that we're making movies for schizophrenics and we'd be out of work before you could say 'boondoggle'. Besides, we're getting a wide enough variation of interpretation just among our supposedly sane working staff."

Teresa was annoyed, but allowed herself to be soothed when Roger approved without question her request for a programmed remote, a self propelled mini-camera.

"How do you know it will be able to transmit back across the integument?" I didn't want to rain on her parade, but skepticism was part of my job description.

"We don't. But in addition to normal transmission, the camera will trail a microfilament wire that will run back through to our side. For all we know, the laws of physics don't work inside the sphere, but even if the experiment fails, we'll have learned something."

The physical link didn't fail. Our minicam transmitted for slightly over three full minutes before its power pack was exhausted. The camera itself was retrieved when the umbilical was retracted, and then we repeated the process and acquired a second recording.

The two versions differed considerably.

Both revealed sprawling landscapes, stretches of level plain dotted with irregular features that could be interpreted as trees, rivers, rocky upthrusts, even buildings and other artificial constructs. Everyone who looked at the two versions had a slightly different impression, and there was clearly considerable variation between the one physically recorded in the camera and the "real time" transmission during the actual probe.

"Could it be a kind of time flux?" Roger had become increasingly uneasy about the subjectiveness of our results.

"Not likely." Teresa sat back, tilting her head to stare at the acoustic tiles in the ceiling. We were all assembled in the small conference room, trying to decide how to proceed. "Not unless time runs differently inside the sphere. And that in itself would mean it's not a part of our universe."

"Not necessarily." Oliver was still wading through the latest printouts. "We don't strictly speaking know that time is a constant within the universe. Earth might well be an exception. Maybe time runs sideways on the other side of the galaxy."

"Look, people, arguing in a vacuum isn't going to get us anywhere. We need hard data." Since Roger was unwilling or unable to take charge, I had assumed de facto leadership. "The question is, how do we go about getting it?"

There were a few seconds of silence before, surprisingly, Roger spoke up. "We need a SCO."

"What?" Teresa obviously hadn't understood the reference, but I'd worked on Project Oz with Roger before coming to Sesame.

"A self contained observer, a SCO. Good point, Roger, but the sphere is only a bit over a hundred millimeters across. We might be able to improve on the camera, but there's a limit to miniaturization of propulsive systems."

"That's right," he said quietly. "We'll have to expand the field first."

There was silence all around the table. I was a bit taken aback myself. Although there was no reason to believe a larger version would be less stable, the very idea was unsettling.

"How much bigger?"

He shrugged. "Ask the engineers. It depends on what configuration would provide the greatest benefit."

"What's the theoretical maximum diameter we can achieve?" asked Oliver.

Teresa thought about it a second before answering. "Theoretically, no upper limit. The energy expenditure increases geometrically though."

"What's the practical limit?"

"About two meters. It would mean running new power lines and refitting most of the hardware, and all of that is going to cost money."

I looked at Roger and, a second later, so did Oliver and Teresa. He sighed. "All right, I'll request a meeting with the oversight committee for a supplementary budget. But don't blame me if the golden goose dies once they notice our existence."

Roger was more persuasive than we'd expected. The funds were approved within thirty days.

I won't bore you with the details of the months that followed. The prototype SCO designed by a subcontracted engineering group failed its preliminary test and cost us two months. Attempts to increase the field size were more successful, although when the diameter reached half a meter, there was a feedback problem that burned out some very expensive equipment. The delays were serious and very frustrating.

As a consequence, we were not ready to proceed for almost a year, by which time we were into the next operating budget, and we'd requested a figure high enough to attract attention. Senator Tyburn, Chairman of the Joint Committee on Scientific Funding, was talking about budget cuts.

"We need results, people, and we need them soon." Roger was clearly worried.

"We're still ten days away from ready," Teresa answered with some exasperation. She'd been working an average of twelve hours a day for several months. She appeared drawn, even haggard.

"We're okay until the end of the month," he conceded. "Congress is in recess. But Tyburn will be on the warpath as soon as it resumes, and I'm told we're number two on his personal hit list. Make things happen, people. Give me something to show the man, or start working on your resumes."

I was expecting disaster on launch day. The SCO was studded with cameras, sensors, recording equipment of every conceivable type. It also carried a powerful microcomputer programmed to follow a preset flight pattern. There'd be no physical link connecting us, and we wouldn't know the results until the SCO was retrieved.

Although I knew the theory as well as everyone else in the room, I still flinched in expectation of an explosion when the SCO hit the sphere. It pierced the meniscus without apparent adverse effect and disappeared inside.

The experiment lasted twenty minutes, although it seemed like hours to those of us watching. There was an audible, collective sigh of relief when our tiny emissary reappeared right on schedule. It was some time later that we learned that there had been a disparity in duration. Several of the devices within the SCO recorded differing elapsed times, as much as thirty three and a fraction minutes, and as little as just under ten.

The last few seconds were crucial. We couldn't trust the perceived landscape to be solid, despite the evidence of our eyes, because that very evidence varied from one observer to another. So instead, the SCO hovered in place, just within the outer surface of the sphere, using the last of its precious store of fuel and reaction mass to achieve a brief moment of stability in an environment where stability itself seemed to be against the laws of nature.

After a moment's hesitation, Robles, one of our best technicians, extended micro-waldoes through the wall of the sphere. They locked onto the SCO which immediately shut down its propulsive system. I was so tense that my nails were pressed deep into the flesh of my palms, and I heard Teresa muttering prayers under her breath as Robles bent to his work.

A moment later the SCO was out and seemed intact.

"Congratulations, folks." Roger's voice shook with emotion. "We've got it."

"Yeah," Teresa agreed. "But what have we got?"

The new data proved to be just as frustrating as the old. Again, different observers had wildly different interpretations, a result that was subsequently confirmed by independent researchers.

It was Teresa who uncovered the truth, or part of it.

I was sitting in the small lounge in the basement of the complex, alone, feeling sorry for myself because Sandy had broken things off. Teresa came in, poured herself a cup of black coffee, and set it down untouched.

"I think we've just changed the entire direction of human history, Nelly." She sounded tired. "I hope it's for the better."

"You're too close to things, Teresa. Most people won't be remotely interested in the sphere, even if they understand what it is as much, or little, as we do. Maybe you need to get away for a few days, get some perspective."

She didn't take offense, didn't even seem to have heard me. "Come on, I want to show you something."

"Can't it wait until tomorrow?" I glanced significantly at the clock.

"Trust me. This is worth your time." So I followed her.

I'd watched the tapes before, many times. As I said, the details changed with every viewing, although the underlying patterns remained the same. Let me explain that. In a given frame, I might see two objects that resembled trees, plus another that appeared to be a small lake. The next time around, it might be two lakes, and a tree, or a tree, a lake, and a large boulder. These are all analogies, of course, since we never actually identified any of the "objects" in a meaningful fashion.

Teresa had taken this as given and concentrated on the background, the setting for the individual features. She'd been particularly interested in the so-called "horizon", the line of demarcation between up and down in the pseudolandscape. For there definitely was a single orientation there; it was just about the only stable factor we'd identified. And the sky was, well, not a sky exactly, more like an ocean of fluctuating forces. It's hard to describe.

Anyway, Teresa had performed an analysis of the curvature of the horizon line, in an effort to determine the diameter of the world we were examining. Her results were provocative.

"It's infinite, Nelly. An infinite plain stretching in every direction."

"That's nonsense. Either your figures are wrong or it's another aberrant reading caused by the limitations of our equipment."

"I can't speak for the equipment, but there's no error in my calculations. The formula is ridiculously simple. I don't doubt the readings either, Nelly. It's really infinite. I know it. I can feel it. And there's something else. Look here."

I followed her to one of the microcomputers we'd slaved to the Superkray. "This is a symbolic representation of the entire landscape taped by the SCO." The screen displayed a rectangle of gray, pockmarked with reversed pixels. "Each of these dots is a mapped feature."

"Very pretty. But what does this tell us?"

"By itself, nothing. But I tasked the computer to compare it to other pattern-whole relationships."

"What in particular?"

Teresa shook her head. "Nothing in particular. That's why it took so long to get results. I put in the request two days ago."

That explained why the system had been so slow to respond lately.

"How did you get Roger to approve that kind of outlay? The access time alone is probably equivalent to our budget for the month."

"Six weeks, actually, and I didn't get his approval. You're the first person I've told about this."

"But..." None of us except Roger had a security level high enough to expend unallocated funds.

"Don't be a child, Nelly," she said with some impatience. "Roger's access code is written on his calendar."

"Teresa, you could lose your job. The cost..."

She didn't let me finish. "Screw the cost. If we don't get results quickly, we're all going to be collecting unemployment. And I've found something, Nelly, I really have."

"All right, show me."

She tapped the enter key and the screen flickered, then remained the same. "See?"

"See what?"

"Exactly. What you're looking at now is NOT the abstract plotting of hyperspace."

"Then what is it?"

"It's a view of our sector of the galaxy, as it would appear from a position roughly eighty degrees skewed above the major axis."

I tried to say something twice, closed my mouth silently both times.

"Now you're beginning to see," she said at last. "That's not a world we're seeing in the sphere. I think it's the entire universe."

It took quite a lot longer to actually convince me, but when I finally left the lab I was too tired to drive, and had to resort to an autocab to get me home. That night I lay awake in bed, imagining spaceships equipped with wheels rolling across that pseudolandscape to reach other worlds in other star systems.

What I've told you up until now is all a matter of record, although the implications have been disguised. Even if the truth was trumpeted in the headlines, most people would yawn, wonder how much it cost to obtain this amusing but useless bit of knowledge, and move on to the sports page.

But there's something else. Something that only I know so far.

The sphere is monitored around the clock, although the equipment is perfectly capable of functioning unsupervised. But the rest of us stop by almost every day as well. The wonder of it all is still a magnetic force.

I let Robles take a coffee break this evening. The landscape inside the sphere was the same as always, which means it varied almost from minute to minute.

A hint of movement caught my eye.

Other than the SCO, we'd never seen anything actually move within the sphere. The shapes we perceived did transform themselves, but it was an almost imperceptible process. This was different; a darker object had changed position just to the right of one of the structures I thought of as broccoli trees, because of their distinctive shape.

I walked to the opposite side, assuming that it had been a trick of the light rather than an actual moving object, but determined to be absolutely certain.

What I saw then didn't even register at first. There was a dark, irregular ovoid that I'd never seen before, in a position where we had never previously recorded an artifact. It moved almost imperceptibly, not the constant shifting of form that I expected but an actual change of position. More importantly, it had extruded a slender, stalklike projection that stretched up above the main body, like an ostrich's neck.

The extrusion reached the concave inner surface of the sphere and passed through, a tiny, budlike object that was turning slowly from right to left, inside the laboratory itself.

I stood in the same position for so long that the muscles in my calves and thighs were rigid cords and I almost stumbled when I finally moved away. The stalk had been withdrawn by then, disappearing into the main body of the...dare I call it the inhabitant of the sphere?

Robles had returned, called my name. I glanced up, tried to talk coherently, choked before taking a deep breath and trying again. "Robles, come over here."

But it was too late; the anomalous shape was gone. It had moved forward over the landscape and disappeared outside the visible range.

I gave Robles some lame excuse or another, and he didn't notice when I programmed the recording devices to dump the evening's recordings into a closed file under my personal password and erase the original material. Don't ask me why I did it. I acted through instinct rather than logic.

This decision is too big for me to make by myself, although I can't imagine leaving it in the hands of politicians. Obviously the field effect we've created is permeable in both directions. We should have realized that when we were able to retrieve our probes. Which means that if we can move from our world to the interior of the sphere, then whatever exists in that plane can accomplish the reverse.

It might be the gateway to the stars. It might be the end of the human race. I can't make decisions like this. The others will be here soon and I'll leave it to them to decide whether or not we should suppress this information and allow the project to be shut down.

God help us if we make the wrong choice.

# AHEAD OF HIS TIME

Darby Lane carried more than a little of the desert on him as he walked into the saloon. Dust and grit matted his hair and covered his exposed skin like a coat of down, and he itched in so many places where it had gotten under his clothes that he'd given up scratching. He'd met a Navajo medicine man once who'd told him to rub his hands with creosote leaves when crossing the desert because it held in the sweat, but he figured he was pretty well insulated as he was.

There were only a handful of people in the saloon even though it was late afternoon. Three men played cards in one corner, and a young woman sat talking quietly to an older man in another. There was a pause in play and conversation as he entered, but both resumed after a second or two. The bartender was a tall, bald man with a sour expression who stood with crossed arms and remained silent until Darby reached the bar.

"Whiskey," he said hoarsely.

The big man barely blinked until Darby took a couple of coins from his pocket and slapped them down on the bar. Even then he looked put upon as he poured from a half empty bottle into a half clean glass and pushed it across the bar's half polished surface. Darby tossed it down, felt his throat clear a little, and gestured for a refill.

"Passing through?" The bartender seemed a bit friendlier now that he was confirmed as a legitimate customer. But not a whole lot friendlier.

"Maybe. Looking for someone." He patted his shirt pocket. "Got a letter offering me a job."

The other man made a derisive sound. "Not much in the way of jobs this side of Silver City. Most of the people round here pulled up stakes and went to dig up a fortune. Damned fools." The derisive snort was repeated. "Two of them already got themselves shot dead and Sheriff Whitehill didn't make himself no friends hiring Dan Tucker as deputy. Sort of like hiring mice to guard the cheese. I told 'em to be patient. The railroad's coming through here pretty soon now. They're thinking about calling this here town New Chicago."

"Well, this here letter is from an old friend." He teased it out of his pocket and frowned at it. It had become frayed as well as dirty and looked so fragile he decided not to open it. "Fellow name of Condon. Alex Condon. I don't suppose you'd know where I could find him?"

"Condon!" The bartender barked a laugh. "We all know Condon, don't we boys?" He had raised his voice and turned toward the cardplayers, who hooted and laughed but never took their eyes off their cards.

Darby waited until the laughter had run its course. "So where do I find him?" He had finished his second drink and let his eyes ask for a third.

This time his glass was filled to the brim. "You'll need a stiffener if you're going out to Condon's place. He's out in the desert a tolerable ride from here." He added some brief directions. "But if I was you, mister, I wouldn't be planning to stay long."

"Why is that?"

"Oh, I think I'll let you figure that out for yourself."

The directions were clear enough and Darby's horse had minimal difficulty picking a path across the rubble strewn desert. The terrain had been less welcoming ever since he'd passed through Albuquerque and by the time he'd reached Socorro he was wondering if this had been such a good idea after all. He and Alex had grown up together in Montana and they'd always been friends, but even then Alex's head had been filled with wildly improbable plans. They were going to find a lost gold mine, or build a giant balloon that would carry them over the mountains, or some such. Admittedly Alex had been clever. Some of his clockwork inventions had been amusing but none had been practical.

They hadn't spoken in years now. Darby had gone south and east, worked at a few ranches in various jobs, was a railroad guard for a year or so, visited Philadelphia and New York and hadn't liked either, then back west where he'd stacked bales of cotton on riverboats, cut wood, even tended store for a while. They'd stayed in touch in a distant sort of way, but sometimes it was a year or more between letters. He knew Alex had gone to California but the Gold Rush was long over and no one was interested in his devices that supposedly extracted gold from marginal strikes. He'd gone up to Canada for a while, then drifted southward into Mexico, the longest gap in their diffident correspondence. Darby hadn't known that his old friend was back north of the border until he'd received the letter offering him a paying job if he wanted it.

Once beyond the small town, Darby had been told that Alex's stucco house was the only raised structure within miles but it blended into the landscape so well that it wasn't visible until he was quite close. The clutter around it, however, was obvious from half a mile away. Clutter was perhaps the wrong word, however, because the odd looking structures were arranged in neatly ordered rows. At first Darby thought they were actually much larger than was the actual case. It was only when he was quite close that he saw that they were individually only about three feet in diameter. But he had no idea what they could possibly be.

Each consisted of a low wooden frame or platform, the top of which was a flat panel of some dark, featureless material. From beneath each of these – and there were at least a hundred – copper wires snaked across the desert floor, intertwining into increasingly thick cables which led to a second adobe building just beyond the first, which Darby had at first been unable to see because of the angle from which he'd approached. There was an obvious clear path through the maze to the larger building but his mount shied nervously at first and only proceeded when Darby leaned forward and clucked reassuringly.

The entire site seemed otherwise deserted until a tall, spindly figure emerged from the second building. At first Darby thought the man must be a Mexican. He wore a wide brimmed sombrero and his skin was dark and worn like aged leather. But then he recognized the perpetual grin and lively eyes that he remembered from his childhood.

"I do believe that's Darby Lane come at last." Alex walked briskly forward to greet him. "I wondered if my letter would even find you, let alone convince you to come."

Darby dismounted and grasped the other man's hand firmly. "Didn't have anything better to do." He glanced around. "Couldn't you have found yourself some prettier country to invite me to?"

Alex shook his head. "Has to be dry for the accumulators." He gestured toward the enigmatic rows.

"And just what the hell are those things? Another one of your inventions, I'd imagine."

"They're the future, Darby. They're going to change the world."

105

"Whatever you say, Alex."

They went inside the larger building, the interior of which looked a lot like Alex's room back when he lived with his parents. There was a bunk bed, the bottom of which was covered with debris – books, papers, drawings, coils of wire, pieces of wood cut to no doubt precise dimensions, discarded clothing, various tools, and other objects Darby couldn't identify. There was only one room, a corner of which had been more or less set aside as a kitchen with a crude table and two chairs, one of which was piled high with books.

"Can I offer you some tequila?"

Darby shook his head. "Just water right now."

Alex retrieved a canteen from what appeared to be a deep hole in the ground, along with a half loaf of bread and a chunk of cheese. "Can't offer you anything better. It's hard to keep food out here. I eat in town mostly. Mrs. Hairston is an able cook. So tell me what you've been doing with yourself."

Darby started to recount his recent experiences, but it was obvious that the question had been courtesy rather than curiosity and he cut it short. "So now I'm here. Would you mind telling me why I'm here and for that matter why you're here?"

It was as if he'd opened the floodgates of a dam. Alex started by explaining that he'd been frustrated by his attempts to convince Californians that burning wood and coal were not the best way to power their steam engines. "The problem is in the availability of sufficient fuel. Riverboats have to stop to take on more wood, the railroads have to have a constant supply of water and coal. That makes them difficult to operate where those resources don't exist, unless they carry them there, which is inefficient."

Darby admitted the point. "But you can't run an engine without fuel."

"Oh?" Alex seemed to dismiss the objection with a single syllable. "A few years ago this Frenchman named Auguste Mouchout powered a steam engine by heating the water by sunlight. It wasn't much of an engine and it only ran for a short time, but the point is that we can trap the power of sunlight and make it work for us. Imagine trains running for days on end without ever having to stop for fuel. We can even power carriages so that they don't need a horse to pull them."

Darby found this last idea rather disquieting, but Alex had frequently disconcerted him with the power of his imagination. "So what does all this have to do with those contraptions outside?"

"Ah, yes. The accumulators. You see, the problem with Mouchot's invention was that it was unwieldy and didn't provide sufficient power. It takes a long time for sunlight to boil water even out here. But you see, it isn't necessary to do that. I use a sort of paste packed between two layers of glass, the top one painted black of course, and pass the energy through copper wires to a specially designed array of batteries I've had built. Come on, I'll show you."

Darby had just managed to get comfortable, having cleared off half of the bottom bunk, but he reluctantly got to his feet and allowed himself to be led outside and into the second adobe hut. In sharp contrast to the first, this one was neat and orderly and as clean as the desert would permit. There were round holes in the walls where the entwined copper cables fed into an odd looking piece of machinery that Alex called his "distributor" that was in turn connected by more copper wires to smaller, cylindrical objects arranged on wooden racks. There were at least a hundred of these. "My batteries," explained Alex. "Much more efficient. They use the same paste as in my collectors. Much better than the old water type."

"So what's this job you had in mind for me?"

"I need to build more accumulators, but unfortunately as the grid becomes larger, I have to spent more time working with the distributor. I have more batteries coming – I have them made special for me in Sacramento – but there's just too much work for one person."

Darby was used to his friend's eccentricities, but this time the scale seemed unprecedented. "How are you paying for all this?"

"Oh, didn't I tell you? My gold detection system worked. I sold the mine, of course. Much too tedious to work it myself. But I'm actually rather rich these days. So how about it?"

They talked a while longer, while Alex tended to his machinery, which buzzed and hissed from time to time until he made minute adjustments. It was only when the sun began to go down that he finally seemed to relax. "What say we go into town and have a big supper to celebrate?"

"Sounds good to me, but I need to clean up."

"You can get a shower at the hotel"

"And a room."

"Nonsense! You can stay here with me. We'll clean that bunk off for you. There's plenty of room."

Darby was dubious, but didn't argue the point.

They fell into their old easy relationship quickly despite the passage of time. Darby built the wooden frames and helped spread the thick paste between the layers of rough glass but Alex insisted on attaching all the leads personally. "If they're not just right, they won't transfer the energy efficiently." They developed a routine, working throughout most of the daylight hours, riding into town most days around dusk for dinner at Mrs. Hairston's diner. Mrs. Hairston also employed four not so young women to provide other amenities but neither Alex nor Darby felt inclined to employ their services.

Sometimes they rode in on horseback, but if Alex needed to pick up supplies – a carton of his special batteries arrived every ten days or so – they hitched up the wagon and used that instead. But Alex had special plans for the wagon. They couldn't carry much cargo because the wagon bed was mostly covered by metal rods and cables and other features Darby couldn't put a name to. Holes had been cut through the wood and some of the cables were loosely attached to each of the axles. Alex refused to explain its purpose, just smiled mysteriously, but every day or so he tinkered with it some more.

Half way through the fourth week after his arrival, Alex announced that they were going to town. Darby glanced up at the sky. "It's not much past mid-afternoon. Why the hurry?"

"Because I've got something special to show you."     Alex headed toward the wagon and Darby started toward the corral to get one of the horses. "No, we won't need them this time."

Puzzled Darby joined his friend who was already climbing up onto the rear of the wagon. "You're driving."

"We're not going far without a horse, Alex." He moved to the front seat, frowning at an upright wooden lever that hadn't been there the last time they'd used the wagon.

"Humor me. Climb up there."

So Darby did, feeling foolish. He glanced back and saw that Alex had attached two of his batteries to the heavy cables installed in the wagon. There was a faint humming that made him feel slightly uneasy. It had never occurred to him that his friend might be serious about a horseless carriage until the wagon suddenly lurched forward a few steps, then came to a stop as the humming faded.

"Hold on one second." Alex adjusted something and the humming returned. They lurched forward again. "Use that lever to steer us."

Darby had already grabbed the lever to steady himself and he found that it shifted with some difficulty to left or right. They were headed directly toward a particularly large stretch of rough terrain so he pulled the lever sharply left. After a second, the wagon began to respond.

It took half an hour for them to work the kinks out. The wagon would have moved faster with a horse pulling it and it was an even bumpier ride, but once Darby got the hang of steering, it felt a good deal less alarming, even exhilarating. He offered to let Alex take over.

"No, I have to stay back here. The mechanism still needs constant tending. I'll get it working by itself sooner or later though."

Their arrival in town caused considerable consternation. Several horses shied away, and a few people did as well. By the time they had reached Mrs. Hairston's, they had accumulated a crowd of nearly half the town's population of three hundred. Some were curious, some laughing, and a few looked frightened or angry.

Alex answered some questions from the onlookers, then offered to buy a round of drinks, which went a long way toward soothing the ruffled feathers in the crowd. The trip home was a lot less successful. They had returned to the saloon for a few drinks after supper and Darby couldn't see very well in the dark and ran them into a shallow gulley where they lost a wheel and were forced to walk the rest of the way back.

Nothing discouraged Alex. "We'll just have to hang a lantern out front when we travel at night. Maybe two of them, one at each corner."

Trouble came a week later. The town's proximity to Mexico had been an advantage during the years Maximilian ruled, but ever since he'd been deposed and executed, there had been near chaos south of the border and it occasionally spilled over despite the aid

President Juarez was receiving from the United States. Bands of conservative recalcitrants, and opportunistic bandits, preyed on any vulnerable targets they could locate, and geography had little to do with their decisions.

Darby and Alex were just about to start shutting down the equipment preparatory to riding into town for supper when they saw a cloud of dust on the horizon. This was not alarming in itself; dust devils frequently danced their way across the flat, dusty landscape. But this particular disturbance did not seem to move at all, except to grow larger, and because of the dimming light it was a while before they realized the import of this phenomenon. The source of the dust was heading directly toward them.

It was too calm to be a tornado. Alex was the first to become alarmed. "I think we might want to arm ourselves."

Darby had barely returned to the outbuilding with their rifles and sidearms when they were finally able to identify the trouble. A group of riders were coming toward them at a brisk pace.

"How many of them, do you think?" Alex strapped on his holster and chambered a round in his rifle.

"Eight or ten, maybe."

His estimate was low. There were at least a dozen, possibly more. They rose in such a close bunch that it was hard to distinguish.

Alex had always been able to talk himself out of tight spots in the past, but he was given no opportunity this time. The bandits opened fire even before they were within range, forcing the two gringos to shelter inside the battery shack and return fire from the doorway. There were, unfortunately, no windows. The raiders drew up short when they reached the outer rim of the accumulators, because they had approached almost directly opposite the open path, which was now swathed in shadows and not obvious. Darby was quite sure he had winged one of them, but they separated quickly and it became much more difficult to fire accurately as they wheeled back and forth, stirring up obscuring dust.

The siege seemed to last for hours but it was probably only a few minutes before Darby turned to his friend. "We can't hold them off much longer. I've already used half my bullets and I haven't hit anything to speak of. Do you suppose we can buy them off?"

Alex shook his head. "They're not likely to accept a draft on my bank account, are they?" He bit his lip. "But I might have an idea. Are you okay here by yourself for a while?"

"Sure. Until they find the way in anyway."

Alex turned away and began busying himself at the controls of his distributor. Darby fired three times at reasonable intervals, not expecting to hit anything but hoping to keep their antagonists at bay.

A hand touched his shoulder. "We're all set."

"For what?"

"I'm going to reverse the process, send all of the stored energy back into the accumulators." He sighed. "Six weeks work lost, and I'll probably burn out some of the wires, but I expect there to be one hell of a flash. With luck we'll blind a few of them. At worst, we should be able to scare them off."

"Well, whatever you're going to do, you'd better do it fast. They're coming through right now."

He was right. They still hadn't found the path in but individuals were picking their way among the rows of accumulators, slowly closing the distance.

"All right," said Darby, withdrawing back into the hut. "When I yell, close your eyes and don't open them for ten seconds."

Darby snapped off another round and knocked the sombrero off one of the raiders. Unfortunately the man's head seemed unscathed. There was a spatter of return fire, some of it from an unexpected direction, and Darby realized the bandits were very close now, penetrating the perimeter at several points.

From behind him, Alex shouted "NOW!" Darby closed his eyes, but even so he was partially dazzled by a burst of radiance brighter than anything he'd ever seen before, and after a few seconds he opened his eyes cautiously, blinking in the glare. The light arced in bizarre patterns, moving across the ground light a living thing. There was a flurry of pops and crackles which he thought at first might be gunshots. It was only later that he realized the painted glass covers of the accumulators were exploding. There was also a sharp cry from somewhere nearby and then a wave of something that had no substance but was somehow material engulfed him, lifted him into the air, and then dropped him to the ground with stunning force.

He sat up in an eerie silence. No one was shooting and the crackles and pops had subsided. "Alex?" He scrambled to his feet and stumbled over something on the ground beside him. It was so dark that he couldn't see a thing but he explored with his hands and discovered a dead body. That gave him a bad moment but it wasn't Alex; the dead man wore a bandolier. One of the bandits then. He raised his voice and called his friend's name again. "What the hell just happened?"

But Alex didn't answer.

Darby groped about until he stumbled into a cactus, then moved more cautiously. As his eyes began to recover, he could make out vague shapes but he felt drained and when he encountered a narrow arroyo, he curled up inside and waited for the dawn.

At first light, he was moving again. There was a town in the distance but it didn't look familiar. Among other things, there was a railroad line running through it. Darby couldn't believe that he'd wandered far enough during the night to reach any other town, let alone one with a rail line, so when he encountered a man on horseback he waved him down and asked the name of the community.

"Elko," was the curt reply and the man moved on before Darby could learn any more.

He reached the town proper a half hour later and discovered that he was in Elko, Nevada, of which he'd never heard. His first thought was that the explosion had addled his wits and that he'd been out of his mind for weeks, but when he inquired about the date, he was astonished to discover that only a single day had passed.

Darby Lane eventually returned to New Mexico but there was so sign of his friend. There was nothing but wreckage where he and Alex had labored for months. No one had any idea where he might have gone, and no one knew what had happened to the bandits either. They had disappeared from the face of the Earth.

Two years later, Darby went home to attend his father's funeral. He felt mildly guilty for having been away so long and decided to stay for at least a few months to help his mother arrange for disposal of the family farm, although as it happened, he never did sell the place. When his mother passed on three years later, he had settled down at last and discovered to his surprise that he enjoyed working the land.

He might not ever have thought of his friend Alex Condon again if he hadn't taken the trip to San Francisco, his first overnight stay away from the farm in five years. He was having his supper at the hotel when he heard someone from the adjacent table mention the name "Alex Condon." Although he thought it was probably just a coincidence of names, he introduced himself and in due course found himself dining with the three men, missionaries recently returned from China.

While visiting that distant land, they had met an American named Alex Condon living in a remote village in the Chinese interior. "Queer duck, he was," said one. "Insisted he was going to discover the secret of instantaneous transportation."

"That's right," said another. "He convinced the locals to let him cover an entire field with these odd box things he'd built. Claimed he was stealing power from the sunlight or some such nonsense."

Darby tried to learn more but without little success. They had not spoken directly to the American. "He has two men working for him and they chase away visitors. Mexicans they were, and I didn't like the look of them."

Darby thanked the men and took his leave and that night he wondered if he would ever see his friend again. Certainly he would never travel to China. But Alex had done so, by whatever means he had inadvertently devised. And if he had gone one way, he could presumably reverse the process and come back.

And if he need, he'd probably have an interesting story to tell.

# COMBAT GOLF

Derek Reiner was as surprised as his fans when he made it into the Masters' Survivors' Tourney with all his faculties intact. Ever since the PGA adopted the new protocols in 2028, designed to increase golf's viability as a spectator sport by adding some physical danger, the word "handicap" had come to have an entirely new meaning in the game.

He drew a deep breath and stepped up to the tee. Today should be the last round despite the storm clouds pouring through the sky overhead. Weather was no longer grounds for suspending play, unless of course it interfered with the cameras. Sammy, his longtime caddy and close friend, handed over the three wood and the scanner.

Derek had simuplayed every hole on this course hundreds, perhaps thousands of times, searching for the optimum strategy to match every combination of wind, air viscosity, coefficient of dew, and temperature. But there were so many potential combinations, so many factors.

After inputting the relevant data through the keypad inset on the grip, Derek waited while the club head adjusted, minor alterations of angle and texture. It wasn't really wood any more, of course; the new multiform synthetics replaced them right after the turn of the century.

In position, Derek held one eye on the scanner until the suddenly gusting wind sank back to within acceptable parameters, then swung the club. He knew it was a good shot even before the telltale on his club flashed a rewarding amber, slightly left of center on the fairway, good distance and placement.

"Nice."

His partner today was Craig Leighton, an old timer playing his fifth and probably final Survivors'. Leighton had clearly lost his concentration this year; he'd stepped on a mine on the fourth hole at Coral Gables early and still hadn't shaken the limp. The fingers he'd lost after picking up a boobytrapped ball two years earlier resulted in a tendency to slice, but he'd learned to compensate well enough to get invited to the last major tournament of the year.

"Thanks. Pool caddies?"

"Sure."

With the two caddycarts moving in tandem, they were able to sweep a wider and more convenient corridor for mines. Modern detection techniques had largely eliminated these as an effective course hazard, but there were still moments of carelessness and equipment breakdowns. Leighton's limp proved that.

The morning went well, despite occasional mild showers and gusting winds. Leighton was far enough back in the standings that he was only playing the round out to keep face, but Reiner was six under par, only two strokes behind Alex Caldwell, the leader and defending champion.

He fell to three back on the tenth hole when his ball took an unexpected hop and ended up in a small pool of acid, a two stroke penalty. On the following hole, Leighton sliced his second shot into a sandtrap.

"Three stroke penalty," Derek said softly. "Bad luck."

"Maybe." Leighton walked to the edge of the trap, stared down at the scorpions scattered across the sand. Then he started to remove his boots.

"What are you doing, Craig? Take the penalty, for heaven's sake!"

"They don't like the rain. I'll be all right."

In order to play out of the sand and avoid the penalty, contestants were required to walk barefoot among the scorpions. Sometimes the creatures ignored the intrusion, other times not. Every one you killed added a stroke to your score.

Leighton's judgment was right until he wedged out. The spray of sand had them moving after that, and he had to crush two with his club head before jumping to safety.

"Still saved a stroke," he said cheerfully.

On the very next hole, Derek was in the rough, but even though he had to take an awkward stance to avoid the poisoned bungee sticks, his recovery shot was spectacular, and he gained a stroke on the leader. An eagle and two birdies later, he was ahead of the field by a single stroke, but Caldwell birdied his final hole while Derek had to be satisfied with par. They ended regular play in a tie.

"Gentlemen, do either of you wish to concede the match at this time?" The referee looked back and forth from Derek to Caldwell. Derek had never expected to face this question, but he'd been playing well above his usual game throughout the tournament.

"I'm in." Caldwell responded quickly, and it was the way he emphasized the first word that pushed Derek to a decision.

"Me too."

The tie-breaker hole was separate from the rest of the course, the only one with artificial turf, necessary to make certain that each player had as equal a chance as possible. The hole was dead center in an oval one hundred feet along its long axis. Derek and Caldwell took their positions in marked boxes at opposite ends, facing each other. The pole marking the hole flashed through its colorful cycle, two seconds each of red, yellow, and green.

"Gentleman, I will now explain the rules." Everyone knew how it worked, but for the benefit of the television audience and to heighten drama, the referee repeated them, the usual stuff about alternating shots in successive rounds until there was a winner. Then came the most important part.

"Remember, a hole scored while the pin is yellow does not count. Only green will count as a valid point. And red, of course," he paused ominously, "is an automatic forfeit."

Derek won the coin toss for first putt and adjusted his stance. The putters were provided to them, old style irons, with no augmentation and no supplementary equipment. Like every professional on the tour, Derek had put in hours practicing for this even though only one player in a thousand ever actually reached this far.

They both missed their first two shots and Derek his third. Caldwell sank that one, but it was in the yellow and didn't count. Then another pair of misses. Derek was sweating, aware that the tension was reducing his concentration, forced himself to breathe evenly as he putted. It rimmed the cup, then fell in just before it turned from green to yellow.

"Point for Mr. Reiner. Mr. Caldwell will now have one shot to answer."

Caldwell took an extraordinarily long time to line up his shot, and the insolent expression had vanished from his face. Derek felt almost sick with tension, and his muscles tightened even further when Caldwell finally hit the ball.

It went straight for the cup, but hadn't been hit quite hard enough. Derek guessed it would lose too much momentum to reach, but he was wrong. It rolled to a stop right on the rim, hesitated, trembling, just as the flag turned yellow. Derek was breathing deeply, trying to realize that he had won the Survivors' Tourney, when the ball finally fell in. The flag was red.

The explosion from the far end of the green was deafening despite the distance. Caldwell's body was lifted into the air by the buried explosives and thrown back toward the viewing area, where he struck the ground and remained motionless. Paramedics were already rushing to his assistance, but only one person had survived a red putt in PGA history, and he had lost both legs and most of his lower intestine.

Derek forced himself to look away, turned in time to accept a congratulatory handshake from his caddy, just as the referee keyed the microphone. "Ladies and gentlemen, will you join me in congratulating Derek Reiner, this year's winner of the Masters' Survivors' Tournament, in a thrilling, overtime finale."

"Sudden death overtime," he whispered, but only under his breath.

# YOUR ENEMY CLOSER

Despite the somewhat lighter gravity on Scrimshaw, Sharri felt as though a great weight had fallen across her shoulders the moment she stepped off the shuttle. It was not the first time she had become discouraged during the past year and would probably not be the last. When she had learned that the man who had killed her father had definitely left Meadow, the thought of finding him somewhere among the hundreds of worlds of the Concourse had been so discouraging that her quest had nearly been stillborn. She had in fact considered using part of her inheritance to buy a new life, a storefront catering to tourists in the capital city of Haven or perhaps a back country farm where she could be alone with her grief and frustration. There was enough credit in the estate to allow her to do whatever she wanted. But anger and resentment had stirred her to action and now she had finally narrowed the search to a single world.

The interior of the spaceport looked very much like the one through which she'd departed Meadow. There were some variations in clothing and hair style and the food being offered at the vending stations looked and smelled different, but the buzz of conversation, the whining of bored children, and the studiously neutral expressions on the faces of the port officials were all the same.

Customs had been taken care of aboard the *Raconteur* and she had arranged for her luggage to be transferred directly to the hotel. Sharri spotted the standard symbol for local transportation and walked down a ramp to a ground level space that opened onto a large courtyard. Through the floor to ceiling windows she had her first look at Scrimshaw, other than the holos she had reviewed during the trip.

Scrimshaw was something of an anomaly. It was one of the oldest human colonies, but it had always been a marginal planet, resistant to terraforming, with too little water to support a robust ecological system and too few resources to command the kind of investment that would overcome that shortcoming. It had not always been that way. Long before humans had arrived, the planet had sported oceans and lush vegetated landmasses but a near miss with some other astronomical body – probably an asteroid – had turned it into a mostly barren wasteland covered with deserts that had once been sea bottoms.

The courtyard made no attempt to disguise Scrimshaw's current condition. It was a garden of sorts, with wide spaced, spiky plants that looked a bit like cactus providing a contrast to a selection of elaborate bone sculptures. Scrimshaw had been a fecund world and its oceans had been filled with giants, giants whose fossilized bones had remained undisturbed until humans arrived and gathered them and arranged them into new and functionally improbable configurations. A good many tourists were lured to Scrimshaw to visit the Bone Palace, Skeleton Falls, and the other major art centers sprinkled across the inhabited zone. She considered it all rather morbid but there was no accounting for other people's tastes.

Sharri summoned a landcab and waited only a moment or two before it arrived. She had expected an autopilot but there was a live human instead, a turbaned man with a dark, wrinkled face and small eyes concealed behind a large pair of opaque lenses who smiled perfunctorily while she was climbing into the passenger compartment. "The Sand Castle, please." He nodded and the vehicle moved smoothly away, slowly at first, accelerating quickly once they were beyond the spaceport's suppressor field.

Sharri had never seen so much sky before. Meadow was not a particularly mountainous planet, but most of its land surface consisted of rolling hills and thick forests. She felt suddenly exposed as they sped across a flat landscape that seemed to extend to infinity in every direction. The interior of the landcab was climate controlled but she could almost feel the heat and light pressing down on them. Scrimshaw was relatively close to its fiercely burning primary and the cloudless sky did little to ameliorate the brightness. At least, she told herself, there would be few dark corners into which Jack Waverly could crawl.

Scrimshaw used the Concourse credit tab as its only official currency, but like most worlds there was an unofficial scrip as well. Sharri had taken the precaution of securing some in advance and she paid her fare and tip with three of the small red bills. The driver's polite smile became perceptibly more genuine and he even waved as she walked beneath an arch of curving bone toward the entrance to the Sand Castle.

It was a tourist trap and she could have gotten similar accommodations for far less credit elsewhere, but the expense was of little consequence to her. Although Sharri had become a very wealthy woman, she felt uneasy in that role. She might have given it all away in a heartbeat to have her father back. Profiting from his death made her feel as though she was an accomplice after the fact of his murder.

The lobby repeated the bone motif ad nauseam. Sharri decided she could get really tired of the décor very quickly. All the more reason to find Waverly as soon as possible. Find him and kill him, of course, preferably in such a way that her involvement would not be known. She had not considered what she would do once he was dead. It felt disloyal to plan her future without first disposing of her obligation to the past. When her thoughts strayed involuntarily to the afterwards, she consciously shunted them into a locked compartment in her mind.

The room was adequate but not luxurious by her standards. Meadow was much more successful attracting offworld visitors and her father had accumulated most of his early fortune making them feel at home, although Sharri had always wondered why they traveled in the first place if that's what they wanted. Her luggage had preceded her, several pieces containing more than she would need even if it took weeks for her to find Waverly. Much of it was camouflage. Some had been shipped in advance; some had accompanied her on the *Raconteur*.

She moved quickly from one case to another, extracting the disassembled parts she had distributed among them. Personal weapons were perfectly legal on Scrimshaw, but they had to be registered. There were sophisticated detection systems designed to spot such contraband, but she had been very careful. The slug thrower was an antique from Lindisfarne and it had cost her a small fortune to have twelve rounds manufactured by hand, rounds which had been enameled and now decorated a garish pendant that she would never have had the bad taste to actually wear. Some of the component parts had been temporarily joined with other, innocuous objects, and it took the better part of an hour before she had it properly assembled, loaded, and concealed once again, but this time intact.

She felt much better then.

Her father and Jack Waverly had been business partners. It hadn't been a long term arrangement. Waverly was an entrepreneur who had developed a plan to divert an asteroid – more of a giant snowball than a rock – and sell water to the habitats orbiting Meadow for considerably less than they were paying to bring it up through the gravity well. All he had lacked was capital and that was something Eldridge Kerk could provide. The partnership had been amicable as far as Sharri knew, but she and her father had been in the midst of one of their frequent estrangements and she had never met Waverly.

The project had been nearly complete when her father had reportedly insisted on visiting the asteroid personally. He and Waverly had gone out in a small skiff, but Eldridge Kerk had not come back. Waverly had spun a reasonably plausible story about a miscalculation in the placement and size of one of the nuclear devices designed to nudge the iceball into a stable orbit, mentioned his partner's questionable decision to view the final course alterations from outside the skiff, and described his desperate efforts to locate Kerk in the midst of a cloud of debris. The authorities had been skeptical but with no hard evidence to contradict Waverly's story, there was nothing they could do about it. The body had never been found.

Sharri had assumed from the outset that it was murder. Her father was too careful, too canny, to have taken an unnecessary risk. And there was ample reason to suspect Waverly's story. The partners had formed a self contained corporation. With Kerk dead, Waverly was entitled to all of the profits, and with Kerk's body missing, there was no way to refute his version of what had happened that day. Sharri had tried to convince the authorities to move against Waverly. He had previously been involved in several questionable projects, her father suffered from mild agoraphobia and would not likely have left the skiff voluntarily, and there was some evidence that it had been Waverly's idea for the two men to visit the site, contradicting his assertion. The prefects had nodded sympathetically, explained that inference was not substantive evidence, and pointed out that Waverly was no longer within their jurisdiction in any case. He had left Meadow shortly after Kerk's death. The bulk of his earnings had gone into an anonymous and ultimately untraceable credit account. Sharri had been clandestinely monitoring his personal account for some time, but there had been no activity, nothing to suggest where he was or what he was doing. Nothing, that is, until a recent charge showed up, originating on Scrimshaw.

"No one ever gets the better of me in a business deal," her father had insisted time and again. But in the end, he'd been outsmarted.

Sharri accessed the planetary net using the terminal in her room, and a quick search revealed no trace of anyone named Jack Waverly. She wasn't surprised. Waverly's checkered past included a few brushes with the authorities and he had been keeping a low profile for some time. That was another reason he'd wanted a partner on Meadow, someone whose name wouldn't raise red flags. He might be here under another name, or he might just have been circumspect about any activity that would impact public records. Sharri had taken similar precautions herself. She was registered as Laralin Dos and had a cloned credit qubit in that name. The real Laralin Dos was back on Meadow, held in status while her new pancreas was being grown.

Sharri was quite sure that Waverly was, or at least had recently been, on Scrimshaw. Somewhere on this dry, worn out world, he might be planning his next enterprise, perhaps choosing his next victim. Sharri was tempted to feel that she was acting for the common good, tracking down a dangerous rogue, but she knew better. She wanted revenge. Waverly had taken her father from her, a treasure whose value she had never realized until it was lost.

Eldridge Kerk had left her more than just memories and a substantial credit line. He had firmly believed in gathering intelligence about anyone with whom he dealt and he had impressed her with the value of adequate intelligence. One of their biggest arguments had followed the revelation that her father was having her watched "for her own good." At the time she had been convinced that it was simply his unwillingness to grant her a life of her own, but she was prepared now to believe that he had acted from habit.

Sharri took a memory stick from her toolkit and plugged it into the terminal. It only took a few seconds to upload her worm, a cyberstalker that would work its way through the barrier between public records and protected data. Her father had possessed a variety of tools not available to the general public. If Waverly was on Scrimshaw, he would have interacted with the planetary net at some point, and her worm would find it.

She ate in the hotel restaurant. The food was dressed up and heavily spiced, but was almost certainly vat grown. There was very little grazing land on Scrimshaw. It didn't matter. Her mind was not on the food and she barely tasted it. When she got back to the room, her worm had already produced results.

It was much better than she had expected. She had hoped to find some fleeting references, perhaps an application for a flitter license. Instead her screen listed more than a score of entries, mostly culled from the Departments of Tourism and Finance. She sat down in front of the screen and began to read.

She was able to piece together a gestalt fairly quickly. Waverly had approached the Minister of Tourism with a proposal to develop a new tourist site to be funded by a partnership between the Hellgate Corporation, Jack Waverly administrator and sole shareholder, and the government of Scrimshaw. Sharri made a face. At least this time he wouldn't be able to eliminate his partner by pushing him out of an airlock. The proposal was to turn an area of uninhabited land surrounding Purgatory Chasm into a resort area. Sharri shook her head. Not the most inventive name. There was probably a Purgatory Chasm on half the planets in the Concourse. There was even one on Meadow.

The project had been approved and preliminary construction was apparently underway. Sharri entered a query about the Chasm itself and skipped through a succession of maps, holograms, and other data. Satisfied that she knew what her next step should be, she cleared the terminal and went to bed.

Purgatory Chasm was several hundred kilometers north of Port City in a largely uninhabited region where low mountains and narrow valleys marked a line between the Great Eastern Desert and the Great Western Desert. The closest settlement was Lord's Rift, population not more than a couple of thousand. There was no regular commercial transportation so Sharri rented a flitter. She had already thought of a cover story and worked out the details during the four hour flight.

Lord's Rift was tucked into the space between two craggy mountains that would have been significant landmarks on Meadow but were pretty run of the mill locally. There was a small flitter park on the edge of town, but the only vehicle there was an older model whose engine compartment was open to the air and coated with grit.

It wasn't quite as hot here as it had been in Port City, but Sharri still winced when she stepped out into the untreated air, adjusting a pair of polarized goggles over her eyes, and strapping a light pack onto her back. There was a lively breeze and a spray of sand stung her face and rattled against the side of the flitter. The chasm would have to be pretty spectacular to lure visitors here, she thought, gazing at the rows of nondescript buildings huddled nearby.

She passed several pedestrians on the way to the commercial district. About half of the men wore turbans, otherwise the two sexes were dressed nearly identically in slacks and blouses with lightweight plasticene jackets. A few gave her curious looks; most did not. There was a kind of beaten down quality to the town that she found depressing. There were no signs on any of the buildings. Presumably all of their customers were locals and the locals knew where everything was. She finally stopped a young woman and asked directions to the prefecture. The woman shook her head. "Prefect Morgan is down with the willies."

"How about his deputy?"

There might have been a shrug. "Morgan's all we've got." The woman moved away, not evasively, just disinterested.

Sharri peered through windows until she found what appeared to be some kind of tavern and went inside. This time she did attract the eyes of everyone in sight, about a dozen evenly divided between men and women. Conversations stopped and she felt uncomfortable breaking the silence.

"Excuse me, but I wonder if anyone here can help. I'm trying to find a man named Jack Waverly."

For a second she thought no one would answer. Some of them exchanged looks, then one man spoke up. "Most likely out at the chasm. Haven't seen him around lately."

"What's the best way to get there? I have a flitter."

There was a flurry of mild laughter. "Can't take a flitter anywhere near the chasm. Air's too rough."

"Can I rent surface transport?"

That generated more amusement. "Rely mostly on leg power here. The sand clogs up engines no matter how careful you handle them."

Another man picked up the thread. "About a kilometer on foot to his office. But might not be in. Spends a lot of time poking around, watching the crews when they're working. Not hard to find but might have to wait a while to see him." He gave brief, clear directions.

She thanked him, bought herself a water bottle and stowed it in her pack.

The wind became progressively stronger for the first half of the trip and Sharri plodded along with her chin on her chest. Then the bulk of the nearest promontory provided some protection and she made better time, although she still had to be careful. The footing was uneven and occasional spurts of air found channels through the crags and buffeted her without warning. The second half of the walk was up a fairly steep incline and she began to feel aches in her calves. Meadow might be primarily an agricultural planet but Sharri had always been a city girl.

She almost walked right past her destination. The project office, which included Waverly's living quarters, was a nondescript building snuggled up under an outcrop. Its walls were so close in appearance to its surroundings that it was hard to tell exactly where the artificial and natural met. Sharri looked around for a touchpad in vain and finally pounded on the door with her fist. There was no answer.

Cursing, she made her way around the side of the building and saw a catwalk leading up and over a barren ridge. There was another building, low and long with no windows and a roll up door, but there was no sign of anyone there either and after poking around a bit, she found a sheltered crevice and settled in to wait.

She was half asleep when she heard someone moving along the catwalk above her. Sharri stood up and stepped away from the sheltering wall of rock. A man was descending toward her but she couldn't see his face. She took another step back and waved to attract his attention. He paused, then returned her wave and quickened his descent. By the time he reached the bottom, she had seen him clearly enough to know that this was in fact Jack Waverly. It had, after all, been surprisingly easy to find him.

She had been imagining this meeting for more than a standard year, had rehearsed a score of scenarios. In each case, she'd announced her identity, sometimes accusing him of his crimes, sometimes merely expressing her profound satisfaction that he would finally pay for her father's murder. The scenarios always ended with his death, usually while begging for his life. Now that the moment was upon her, she realized that all of those fantasies were just that. For one thing, if she took the slug thrower out of her pack and shot him, she would almost certainly be apprehended before she could leave the planet. She'd been seen in the town asking for him and there was a record of the flitter rental. They'd think they were arresting Larilin Dos, of course, at least at first, but it wouldn't matter to her what name they used.

There was a second problem that she had never anticipated. Sharri had no doubt that she was capable of killing a man, particularly this man, but a perfunctory assassination now would feel anticlimactic. It would be over too soon and then she'd have to face that indistinct future that she'd locked up inside her mind. No, it would be much more satisfying to know more about Jack Waverly before she revealed herself to him, and avenged her father. This wasn't just an execution; it needed to be personal.

"Hello, I'm Laralin Dos. You must be Jack Waverly."

He shook her hand somewhat warily. His face was unmistakable but his physical presence was not what she expected. She felt intimidated. Sharri told herself it was just nerves but she knew it was more than that. Waverly was naturally dominant. It was a quality she recognized. Her father had possessed the same ability to project confidence and authority. "Yes, I must. What brings you way out here?"

Her cover story fell into place. "Business. I have a proposition for you."

Waverly stared at her appraisingly for a second, then nodded. "Come inside and tell me about it"

The interior was not at all what she had expected. It was neat, orderly, and fairly clean although it was clearly impossible to keep all of the sand out. The furniture was minimal and functional but Waverly had somehow managed to suggest taste and even comfort if not luxury. The front room was obviously businesslike with a desk, net terminal, a few chairs, and pictures on the walls, mostly of seascapes. There was a loft that obviously functioned as living and sleeping quarters.

Waverly insisted on preparing cold drinks for the two of them and disappeared through a doorway into the back, giving Sharri adequate time to look around. She had always pictured Waverly as living in seedy quarters that reflected the blackness of his soul. Her father had always warned her against making quick judgments of people. "Always assume that the other guy is holding something back, hiding something. The things we keep secret are more important than the things we make public."

The drink was good, fizzy but not too sweet. Waverly settled behind his desk. "Now what exactly can I do for you?"

Sharri delivered her spiel, almost exactly as she had rehearsed it. Her proposition would pass muster. Her father had insisted that she learn the hotel business and despite her resistance enough had stuck to make her new persona plausible. "My understanding is that you're planning a high end resort. I would like to complement it with a less expensive facility that wouldn't compete for your customers but would increase traffic overall. Of course, I'd be willing to consider a reasonable royalty in addition to whatever we decide upon for licensing and the lease of the land."

Waverly asked a few questions which she fielded without difficulty. He clearly had reservations but had not rejected her proposal out of hand. She was careful not to sound too eager. "This is all contingent upon the successful implementation of your development plan. My backers aren't going to risk their capital until they're confident that Purgatory Chasm is a viable investment opportunity."

"Would you like to see the chasm itself?"

The question caught her by surprise. Actually she hadn't the slightest interest in poking around in a hole in the ground, but it would not be consistent with the character she had created to turn down the offer. "At some time when it is convenient, yes, I would."

Waverly abruptly stood up. "No time like the present. If you're up to a bit of climbing, that is."

She pressed her lips together. There was no way that she would admit weakness in front of this man. "All right. But I do need to find lodging for the night. It's a long way back to Port City."

"There's a transient station back in the Rift. It's pretty basic, I'm afraid."

"I've probably stayed in worse."

Waverly led the way back to the catwalk. She followed him up the side of the ridge, then across an open rock face to a second walkway. "Clip on to the guard rail." Waverly was already attaching an electronic tether to his belt. It was strong enough to support his weight, smart enough to transmit a distress call if his body pulse or body temperature warranted an alert. "The walkway is sturdy enough but we often get heavy gusts near the rim."

Sharri found a second tether and secured herself. They were quite close together now and she felt uneasy. Waverly had a way of looking at her that was unsettling, as though he was peering into her very being. She stepped away and peered forward, but the lip of the chasm was gradual and she couldn't see much from where she stood. "Just how deep is it?"

"Well over a thousand meters to the lowest point. There's a deeper one on the other continent, but the view there isn't as spectacular. Ready?"

The chasm was much more impressive than she had imagined. Even the intense sunlight had trouble penetrating into its depths and Waverly used a remote to turn on banks of lights from time to time as they descended. "Only about ten percent of the lighting is currently in place. That's my main priority once construction resumes."

Sharri had noticed that they were alone. "Is this a holiday? I expected to see a construction crew hard at work."

Waverly shook his head. "No, I'm waiting for the bureaucrats to come through with the first installment of their share. I could keep going using my own resources but that would just encourage them to stall even longer."

The interior of the chasm grew more spectacular as they descended. Twisted, gnarled extrusions poked out from the walls in terrific profusion, intertwining at times like a coral reef without the water. The predominant color was deep carmine but there were yellows and blues and greens scattered through them as well. Some of the configurations looked like claws or even grasping hands. "What is this stuff?" she asked at last.

"Originally, some kind of marine growth, like a barnacle. When the oceans went away they adapted to the drier environment. The surface is actually quite porous. They filter water out of the air and draw solids from the rock walls and from each other."

Waverly called a halt when they were approximately two hundred meters down. "This is far enough. The climb back isn't nearly as easy."

Sharri felt a twinge of disappointment; she had wanted to see more. "How are you going to get your customers to trek all the way down here and back?"

Waverly shook his head. "I'm not. There's going to be a bubble rail. That's a fabrication shop behind my quarters. I can turn out custom made sections for a tenth what it would cost to import them. In fact, I plan to make most of my equipment on site, except for delicate electronics. Once the rail is in place, tourists will be able to rent a capsulecar and sit in comfort while they travel down into the depths of Hell itself. If you look closely, you can see a section of rail over there behind that promontory. We're trying to keep it as unobtrusive as possible."

"How will you manage the installation without damaging the scenery?"

"With difficulty, I'm afraid. We lower the sections with cranes mounted on the rim, then Quikfix them to the walls until the permanent fittings are in place."

"What's Quikfix?"

"It's a temporary adhesive rigid as metal when it's activated but after eight hours it begins to break down. After twelve, it turns to a flaky ash and dissipates. It only takes four to six hours to install the permanent bonding so that gives us plenty of time."

"This could be a gold mine, you know." She wasn't play acting now. There was enough of her father in her to recognize that this could be a very profitable enterprise. "I may be able to convince my backers that they should make a bigger commitment than we anticipated. If you're open to outside investment, that is."

Waverly smiled. "We can certainly talk about it."

And talk they did, for several days. Sharri commed the Sand Castle and had her clothing shipped out by droplifter. The transient house was Spartan but she had her own room. Sometimes she trekked out to the site for the day; sometimes Waverly came into the Rift and they commandeered a table in the tavern. Their host was more than hospitable.

"They see me as the town's salvation," explained Waverly. "This has been a marginal settlement all along, but if the resort opens up, there'll be plenty of jobs and lots of credit floating around."

Sharri told herself that she was just biding her time, establishing a plausible relationship, waiting for an opportunity to kill Jack Waverly in such a way that he would know who was responsible and why, without leaving any hints that might give the authorities the same idea. In fact her feigned enthusiasm gave way to the genuine article. Waverly had developed a comprehensive, innovative, and potentially very profitable business plan. A new idea began to evolve in her mind, a way to doubly avenge her father.

"Any sign of the government moving on their share of the investment?" she asked one afternoon.

Waverly shrugged. "They claim that everything is proceeding smoothly but no, they haven't ponied up yet."

She took a deep breath. "I've spoken to my primary backers and they're prepared to step forward on this."

They were in his quarters, eating an undistinguished lunch, and Waverly raised his head, chewing slowly. "What does that mean, precisely??"

"We're offering to match your investment credit for credit, conditional upon the exclusion of the government of Scrimshaw from the process."

"You want to take over their half of the outlay?"

She nodded. "In return for their half of the profit, of course."

"That's an interesting idea." He sat back in his chair. "I suggest we discuss it over a bottle of wine."

It took two bottles of wine to work out the outline of an agreement, after which Sharri was not steady enough to walk back to the Rift. Fortunately, Waverly's bed was large enough for two.

It was easy to find excuses to delay exacting her revenge after that. Sharri discovered that she had a natural ability for management, another legacy from her father. But Waverly was a driving force, energetic, magnetic, and persuasive. He demolished obstacles with an ease that she envied. She thought that the young Eldridge Kerk must have been a lot like Jack Waverly, then dismissed the thought as disloyal. Her father had been nothing like this man. Waverly was a murderer. But he was also a marvelous lover. She would feel a twinge of regret when she finally killed him.

At her suggestion, they had entered into a self contained partnership very similar to the one he had shared with her father.

Waverly had expressed surprise when she proposed the arrangement. "Won't your backers object? They'll have no legal right to their shares."

"They prefer to remain anonymous for reasons of their own. And they've taken appropriate measures to safeguard their interests."

Waverly seemed to find this amusing, but had not raised any objection. Sharri had no intention of becoming his next victim so she was very careful to control the flow of investments. She would be safe at least until Waverly had the resources to complete the project on his own.

The construction crews were housed in a temporary camp near the Rift. The main resort would be close by and that's where the bulk of the work was underway. The bubble rails were put in place as quickly as they could be fashioned, except when deliveries of Quikfix were delayed, as they often were. Sharri spent a lot of time watching the engineers draw up templates for the fabricators. They were more than happy to show an attractive young woman how the process worked, even let her design and create a crude bracelet.

If she'd been honest with herself, Sharri would have admitted that she was having the best time of her life. She began to appreciate her father's fondness for steering massive projects to completion. The work was itself the purpose rather than the profits. The profits only mattered because they could be used to finance the next project. There were even times when she forgot that her partner was the man she was determined to kill. He was charming, intelligent, and a thoughtful lover. It was a shame that it was necessary for him to die.

And that moment drew closer with each passing day.

As the work neared completion, Sharri considered various options. She was sharing Waverly's quarters by then so there was ample opportunity. It was necessary that his death appear to be accidental, but Waverly also had to see it coming and know why it was happening. And so she made her plans and made her preparations.

One evening, after the workers had left for the day, she suggested they go for a walk. "Down into the chasm," she insisted. "We've been so busy I haven't actually looked at it in weeks."

Waverly had seemed reluctant but had agreed. They took the same catwalk that they had used the first time they'd met, although there was now a network stretching around the interior of the cavern.

These would all be removed once the last of the bubble rails and the emergency lifts were in place. As they descended to the place she had chosen, Sharri became depressed. Despite everything, she liked Waverly, and the elaborate charade she had engineered was the most fun she had had in her adult life. But he had murdered her father and it had to be set right.

At last she reached the spot she had chosen and removed the slug thrower from the pocket of her jacket. "Stop right there, Jack."

He turned to face her, and one eyebrow rose to indicate surprise, but not a lot of it. "What's going on?"

"I need to tell you a few things. First of all, my name isn't Loralin Dos."

He nodded. "I know that. You're Sharri Kerk and you think that I murdered your father."

Her hand shook, just perceptibly. "How long have you known?"

"Almost from the start. You didn't think I'd take on a business partner without doing a little research, did you? Loralin is still waiting for her pancreas to mature. But I knew you were lying to me the first time we met."

Sharri bit her lip. "Was I that transparent?"

"No, actually you were pretty good. Your father's daughter, in fact. He was a fine actor himself. He was very fond of you, kept a holo on his desk all the time, insisted on pointing it out every time we met."

"Oh," she said softly. "Then you know what I have to do."

Waverly shook his head. "You don't have to do anything, Sharri. You think you want to kill me, but you really don't."

"Don't I?"

"You have no reason. I haven't harmed you in any way."

Fury flared and her hand steadied. "You killed my father. Isn't that enough reason? Or are you still going to claim that you weren't responsible?"

Waverly seemed almost to relax. "No, you're right. I did kill Eldridge Kerk, but it's not what you think. I had no choice. He was trying to kill me."

"That's a lie! He would never do something like that!" But she wasn't as certain as she wanted to be. Her father had been a relentless competitor and had often used shortcuts, not always legal ones, to get what he wanted. There had been rumors about some of his activities but she had chosen not to believe them.

"It was your father's idea to visit the site. I would have been perfectly happy leaving everything to the hired help. When we got there he insisted that we go outside to take in the magnificent view. While I was busy he started back toward the airlock, intending to lock me out and abandon me, but I'd already become suspicious and had changed the entry code. He tried to make it around the hull to the emergency lock but there was a premature detonation on the asteroid and we were dangerously close. I never saw what happened but one of the fragments must have hit him. I did look for him but it was hopeless."

Sharri let her arm drop part way so that it pointed at Waverly's knees. "Why should I believe you?"

"No reason in particular. Maybe just because you know me well enough to recognize when I'm lying and when I'm telling the truth."

"Dad had a ruthless streak, and it got worse as he got older." Her voice wavered. "I suppose it could have happened that way."

Waverly hadn't seemed tense, but now he visibly relaxed. "I know it's difficult to accept. Your father told me how close the two of you were."

Sharri smiled and her arm came back up, the slug thrower pointed directly at Waverly's face. "Dad and I detested each other, Jack. Didn't you wonder why you and I never met? And your thrilling survival story doesn't hold water either. He was terrified of open spaces. Did you drag him kicking and screaming out of the airlock or was he already dead by then?"

For the first time, Waverly appeared uncertain of himself, even worried, but the old confidence returned almost immediately. "I killed him first. Painlessly. It wasn't easy getting him into an environmental suit afterwards but I managed, just in case someone came across the body. I had intended to send it down to the asteroid to be vaporized in the explosion, but I was telling the truth about the premature detonation. One of the fragments almost hit the ship." He folded his arms across his chest. "But what do you care? His death made you rich and if you really did dislike each other, it must have been a relief to have him out of the picture. I did you a favor."

"Maybe, but one thing Dad taught me is that Kerks always collect on their debts. That's why I waited so long. You've committed just about every credit you own to the Purgatory project, and with your death, I become the sole shareholder. Appropriate, don't you think?"

"Very neat. Too bad it's not going to work."

She cocked her head to one side. "Oh? And why is that?"

"The first night you spent at my place, I drugged your wine. While you were sleeping it off, I went through your pack and removed the firing pin from your weapon." He nodded toward the slug thrower. "You might as well be holding a rock."

Sharri smiled, shifted her aim to one side, and pulled the trigger. There was a sharp crack and then a whine as one of the slugs careened off an outcropping. Waverly's eyes widened. "Dad always said that you can't check things out too often. I fabricated a replacement part a long time ago."

Waverly's face showed no expression but she could sense the cogs whirring behind the calm façade. "They'll recover my body and know it wasn't an accident. Are you really willing to give up your own life just to take mine?"

Sharri smiled. "You mean because of this?" She waved her weapon at him. "This was just to make you behave during our little talk. I'm not going to shoot you."

The look of sudden uncertainty in Waverly's eyes brought a smile to her lips, but he was quick on his feet. He'd risk charging toward her at any moment now. It was time to end the game. She reached into her pocket and touched the remote. Waverly jerked as though he'd touched a live electric line, then collapsed, unconscious. The tether, convinced by her signal that the man was in excruciating pain, had administered an anesthetic, but she had disabled the automatic distress signal.

For a few seconds she couldn't find the package she'd secured beneath the catwalk, but then her questing fingers found the cable and she hauled up the compact package. Waverly should be out for the better part of an hour, but she wasn't taking any unnecessary chances. She wrapped multiple strands of Quikfix around his body, forming a virtual cocoon, secured the two loose ends to the guard rail, then triggered the reaction that turned it into a rigid cage.

She had more trouble than she had expected pushing him between two of the uprights but she persisted and when his fall was caught short, the entire catwalk shook violently. She had a sudden vision of it tearing loose and carrying them both down into the depths, but it held, as did the Quikfix.

Sharri was alternately dazed and elated as she walked back to the Rift, reclaimed her flitter, and set it on auto to carry her back to Port City. She wanted to be some place very public when the Quikfix lost its tensility and relinquished its grip on Waverly, who should be fully awake by then.

The investigation was perfunctory. Sharri had mentioned to several of the workers that Waverly had a penchant for wandering around the chasm after hours and often failed to secure himself with a tether. "I know he's perfectly safe but sometimes it worries me." There was no secret that Waverly's shares were subsumed into the corporation, but Sharri had maintained her cover identity as Larilin Dos and Dos had nothing to gain from Waverly's death. Of course, Sharri Kerk had a great deal to gain, but no one could suspect her because she was back on Meadow, still grieving for her father. Everything had gone according to plan.

Which made it even more surprising when the prefecture summoned her to Port City for an interview.

She was ushered into a plainly furnished room occupied by two men and one woman. The woman introduced herself as Prefect Kurosev. "Please have a seat, Miss Kerk."

Sharri was startled to be addressed by her real name but was confident it hadn't shown in her face. At least not much. Discovery had always been a possibility and she had planned for it. "I was afraid someone would find out who I was." She sat.

"Would you care to explain why you are using a false identity?"

Sharri had rehearsed this moment as well. Her story would hold up. It was not uncommon for entrepreneurs to create alternate egos to disguise their involvement in certain business ventures. It was not even technically illegal although she supposed in this case Larilin Dos could file an action against her for misappropriating her identity. Kurosev listened politely, her face expressing neither acceptance nor skepticism.

"Would you care to describe your relationship with your former partner, the late Jack Waverly?"

She did so, truthfully, even volunteered the information that Waverly and her father had been partners, but left out anything incriminating. "Dad thought very highly of his abilities."

"But you said you initially approached him without identifying yourself."

"I wanted to evaluate him personally beforehand. And once I felt reassured, I told him the truth."

Kurosev smiled. "That's not precisely how Waverly describes the situation."

Sharri frowned. What was the woman talking about? Jack Waverly was dead, wasn't he? "I'm afraid I don't understand."

"No, you wouldn't." Kurosev began tapping the table with her fingers. Then she sat back and explained. Waverly had recorded his own version of events in a file which had resided quietly on the planetary net. When Waverly had failed to perform a periodic task, the file had commed itself to the Prefecture in Capital.

"Your father died in the company of Mr. Waverly, didn't he?"

"Yes," she admitted. "But that was an accident."

"Was it? Not according to Waverly. He insists that you became lovers while he was in the Meadow system, that the two of you conspired to murder your father. Waverly became sole shareholder in the Iceball Corporation, while you inherited the larger part of a substantial fortune."

Sharri leaned forward, her mouth open to refute the charge, but Kurosev ignored her. "He also asserts that the two of you agreed not to communicate with each other for a standard year to allay any lingering suspicion, and then to reunite here on Scrimshaw. He was somewhat disheartened to find that during the interim, you had grown even harder and less susceptible to his charms, and he was afraid that history was about to repeat itself. As it has."

This time it was Kurosev who leaned forward. "By the authority of the Prefecture of Scrimshaw, I am detaining you on suspicion of the murder of Jack Waverly. I'm aware that you appear to have an alibi but I'm sure we'll find out how you managed things once we have you under Truthtell." She glanced at the two men. "Please convey the prisoner to her new quarters." Then she turned back to Sharri.

"Don't worry, Miss Kerk. If you feel the need to talk about it, I'll always be close by."

# MARTYRS

Pennington contemplated the nature of self sacrifice as she watched several male sandrunners feverishly biting off their own legs in their haste to be the first to enter the queen. Her swollen body was so full of unfertilized eggs that she looked more like a rough textured balloon than a living creature, and although her mass was so low that Pennington could easily have picked her up and pitched her further out into the desert, she could potentially give birth to several thousand offspring, most of whom would enjoy a lifespan limited to a few hours. Her own limbs had atrophied and even the beetle-like head had receded until it was only the largest irregularity on her blotchy, scaly exterior. The entrance to her sex was prominently displayed, but the narrow opening could just accommodate a single male, and even then only after the lucky suitor had severed his own limbs and squirmed inside, where he would slowly inseminate the surrounding eggs while his own body was equally slowly digested by his mate.

The other males, bereft of their limbs, would die more quickly, of course.

She turned away when she heard the door open behind her. It was McNabb, who always slept late and then was impatient to be on the move. As usual the xeno-anthropologist was dressed like something straight out of a holo from old Earth, complete with a wide brimmed, heat resistant hat and a state of the art, bio-responsive bodysuit that was designed to monitor its wearer's vital signs and make minute environmental adjustments as appropriate. Pennington didn't trust machines that thought they were smarter than she was, even the ones that demonstrably were. Besides, unaugmented clothing rarely malfunctioned. One of her clients had almost been roasted by his own biosuit when the sensors malfunctioned and tried to compensate for subpolar cold in the middle of a heat wave.

"Another one, huh?" McNabb nodded toward the sandrunner queen. "Why do you find those damned things so fascinating?"

"It's mating season," said Pennington, ignoring the second question. "They've been rolling their queens over the sand for months and they're anxious for their reward. It's the only pleasure they'll ever experience."

"But only one of them gets that honor, if you call being slowly eaten alive rewarding."

Pennington shrugged. They'd been together long enough now that she was hypersensitive to her client's prejudices. For a self proclaimed seeker after truth, McNabb seemed convinced that he already knew what it was. "It must be worth it or they wouldn't do it."

"So if they all bite their own legs off, how do the survivors bury the old lady in the sand when the wedding is over with?"

"The survivors don't." Pennington turned away from the sandrunners, picked up her pack and slung it over one arm. "Only the strongest of the males get to compete for her favors. The rest will be along after they finish foraging for the day. They'll cover her over except for the breathing sacs, then take turns standing guard for the next season. When they're ready a new generation will come churning up out of the sand, ravenous, and their first meal will be their dear old uncles, all of them. Then the females fight to the death, the last one alive is promoted to queen, and the cycle starts all over again."

"Sounds more like a machine than a living creature." McNabb already wore his pack, and he followed Pennington to the crawler.

She couldn't resist the temptation to poke at him one more time. "They're a lot like us when you stop to think about it. Millions of humans have died in service to their nation or the race at large, or at least that's how they rationalized their sacrifice at the time. Why does it have to have a point? Why can't it just be the way things are?"

McNabb didn't answer. He refused to be drawn into an intellectual debate with someone who lacked the proper credentials, both academic and gender specific. He was an anachronism, which explained his career long preference for field work in remote locations like this one. Pennington also did a background check on her clients and she knew that his career had proceeded by fits and starts. He would light some place – a university or a research group, quickly alienate everyone in sight, and then his contract wouldn't be renewed or he'd be quietly asked to leave on some pretext or another. His published papers were frequently acerbic and often controversial.

They didn't speak as they stowed their packs in the back of the crawler and climbed into the front. Pennington had recharged the primary energy cell and checked both backups while McNabb was still asleep. Grogan Station was the last human outpost they'd visit during this trip, unless you counted the abandoned camp at Teardrop, the dig site.

"At least we humans rise above our instincts from time to time. We're not so firmly caught in the trap of biology. Instinct has to give way to reasoned analysis."

A few seconds passed before Pennington realized that her companion was responding to her own previous remark. She suppressed a smile, delighted that she had managed to get under his skin. "I don't know. Maybe it's just that our particular trap is so subtle that we don't realize we're caught."

McNabb made a noncommittal sound. "That's a cheap argument, since by its very nature it's irrefutable. I suppose you could say we're trapped by our own mortality, by the physical limitations of our fleshy containers, but at least we're trying to achieve more than simple self replication. Most of us will live twice as long as we would have a few centuries ago."

"Moving to a larger cell doesn't get us out of the prison."

McNabb laughed humorlessly as Pennington started the crawler's engines.

In many ways, Ochre was one of the most hospitable planets humankind had discovered. Its atmosphere was so close to optimal that breathing equipment was unnecessary except in a few mountainous regions. There were no dangerous predators, not even unpleasant bacteria, and the weather – though it varied considerably between equator and poles – avoided serious extremes. Even the deserts were tolerable for most of the year. But even though the water was safe to drink, there was no food native to Ochre which would nourish the human body. It might fill a person's stomach without poisoning them, but they'd starve to death in the midst of apparent plenty. Efforts to introduce more useful flora and fauna had been intermittently successful but the ongoing support required to maintain an introduced ecosystem within the native biosphere was not economically viable. Had it not been for the widely scattered ruins of an extinct alien civilization, Ochre might have been abandoned entirely. There were other planets much more amenable to human colonization, or which contained rewards that justified extraordinary efforts.

Pennington was not a recluse but neither was she particularly garrulous. Most of the previous parties she had guided into Ochre's desert had consisted of small groups of scientists who spoke mostly among themselves, treating her politely but firmly as hired help. There had been some casual flirting but nothing she couldn't fend off amicably enough. Her craggy, windburned face discouraged most of her male clients and her height and obvious fitness discouraged the rest.

She had guided parties of scientists and explorers and even the occasional tourist and she never took offense when she was treated almost as though she were just another piece of equipment, excluded from planning sessions unless someone had a question she might be able to answer. As long as her fees were paid, snubs were of no consequence. McNabb had in fact surprised her by talking about his research persistently right from the outset, shouting much of the time because the crawler was an older model, its engine badly needed adjustment, and the rumbling vibration drowned out normal conversation. But McNabb was the first party of one she'd ever dealt with, and McNabb had no one else to belabor.

Pennington had been favorably impressed for the first half day, at which point she had realized that her part of the conversation was intended to be a succession of endorsements of McNabb's opinions. The fact that she probably knew as much or more about the Ochran ruins than he was not a factor in their intercourse. Once she recognized that she was to be an echo rather than a sounding board, she slipped into that role easily. She'd worked with fools before. Their money was just as good as that of wiser men. If McNabb had noticed her change of attitude, he gave no sign.

It took a long time for the station to disappear behind them, not because they were moving slowly but because this part of the desert was unusually flat and featureless. There was actually quite a lot of vegetation, but most of it consisted of variegated water gatherers with broad leaves spread flat against the ground, the edges turned up to retain any condensation or precipitation that might gather there. Rain fell several times annually, but never hard enough to quench the thirsty soil. A plume of dust rose behind them as they moved across the wasteland, slowly settling in their wake as though annoyed at having been disturbed.

They normally ate while they traveled, but Pennington took advantage of a shady ravine to stop for their mid-day meal. Although McNabb was oblivious to any aspect of his environment that held no interest for him, she had a more practiced ear and knew the crawler's engine needed attention. Sometimes the desert sand, which was unusually fine in this region, infiltrated the protective seals and lodged in places meant to be free of obstruction. A few minutes maintenance now was preferable to a comprehensive cleanup later, so she ate her rations quickly and used the powervac while McNabb investigated the partially fossilized skeleton of some prehistoric sea creature that protruded from the sand. Ochre had undergone dramatic changes during its lifetime and the ocean that had at one time covered this part of the planet was long since gone.

It was the hottest part of the day, but Pennington was barely sweating. She had lived on Ochre for most of her adult life. On the other hand, despite his state of the art outfit, McNabb's skin was covered with a sheen of perspiration. He had complained about the heat constantly the first two days, and intermittently ever since.

"What is this thing?" McNabb asked, his foot tapping the lower end of a gently curved rib that arched up and over his head.

Pennington didn't even glance in his direction. "It's not likely anyone's gotten around to naming it. Some kind of oversized fish. This used to be an ocean, you know."

"Really?" It was not the first time McNabb had been openly sarcastic. "I never would have guessed."

Pennington chose to pretend she hadn't noticed his tone. "I'm about finished here." She closed the engine compartment, tapped the containment icon. There was a whisper of compressed gas as the seals activated. "Ready to go?"

As flat as the desert had appeared, they had been climbing a very gradual rise for the past two hours and were now at its crest. Distant features to their rear disappeared quickly as they moved onward and new ones debuted ahead. Pennington knew the route intimately, but she still paused to take her bearings and make sure she was right where she thought she was. They were in no real danger, even if they got lost, since they could always radio for help, but it would be embarrassing as well as expensive, and her career as a guide would potentially be in serious jeopardy. She had a good reputation but the influx of new clients had slowed dramatically over the course of the last two years, and it was getting harder than ever to pay the bills. She owned her little homestead free and clear, but she had to buy food from the hydrofarms and fuel from the port authority. Both of these were on a cash only basis.

She had just adjusted their course westward when McNabb raised his voice to a low shout. "Do you really think a rational person would die to benefit someone else?"

Once again McNabb had reverted to a conversation Pennington had thought concluded, but this time she picked up the thread right away. "I thought someone in your profession would be familiar enough with human history to make that question unnecessary."

"Oh, I don't deny that there are numerous cases of self sacrifice. I question the motive. When a believer dies rather than deny his or her god or country or political persuasion, is that individual truly motivated by a wish to help others or is it just a kind of hubris? Martyrs all seem to have an excess of ego and usually a penchant for the theatrical. They're playing up to an audience. If there was no one around to be impressed by their nobility, they'd change their principles in a minute."

In that case, it seemed to Pennington, McNabb was a prime candidate for martyrdom. He didn't seem to believe in anything except perhaps his own importance. The conversation held no interest for her. McNabb only listened to her opinions in order to refute them. It was a reflex, she suspected. "I don't suppose we can ever know what goes through a person's mind at that moment," she said mildly, but McNabb wasn't paying attention. Instead he'd wandered off on a fresh tangent of his own.

After a few minutes of welcome silence, he turned to look at her. "I suppose that if I found myself facing unavoidable death, I'd try to put a good face on it and claim that I was giving my all for some cause or another, but truthfully I'd rather live to fight another day, as would any reasonable person. Or live just for the sake of living. I certainly wouldn't voluntarily give up my life, no matter how noble the justification. Once you've stepped off the boat, it really doesn't matter to you if it sinks."

"So there's no situation in which you'd die to save someone else, or even to uphold a principle?"

This time McNabb chose to hear her, had perhaps hoped she'd provide the opening for a riposte he had already worked out in his mind. "Of course not. Tell me, Pennington, would you give your life for me?"

Pennington paused, as if considering the question from every point of view, though in fact she was trying to anticipate where she was being led. "No," she said at last, drawing the syllable out. "Not for you." She turned to face him as she spoke, her expression carefully neutral.

It was probably the answer he had expected because it seemed to support his position, but something in her delivery disquieted him. For the first time since they'd met, it was McNabb who seemed out of his depth. He laughed uncomfortably, shelved the rest of his prepared argument for another occasion, and turned away to look out across the rolling landscape. Pennington smiled to herself and felt better than she had all morning.

Late that morning they ran into a colony of longtrekkers. At first glance, longtrekkers appeared to be mammals. Their bodies were covered with a coast of bristly fur and they had a spatulate tail that trailed behind them in the sand. On average they were the length of a forearm but their bodies were quite narrow, the knobby, armored head tucked into a declivity between the shoulders. Nictitating membranes covered the eyes, which were many faceted and quite large, but the ears were almost vestigial, just bare spots on the sides of the head.

Despite appearances, they were more like insects crossed with reptiles. They were cold blooded, lived in underground colonies that resembled anthills, and they reproduced asexually, the predominant method on Ochre. Concealed within their mouths were filament like suckers which they used to draw moisture out of the earth as they expanded their tunnel system. They were also known as waterminers on the southern end of the continent, but out here in the desert they were longtrekkers, named as such because when they exhausted the potential of an existing colony, they abruptly abandoned it and crossed the desert en masse, driven by some unknowable instinct, until they found a new location that satisfied them. Along the way at least half their number would perish and their bodies would be scavenged by the others, drained of all liquids and nutrients, so that the migration could continue.

MacNabb objected when Pennington stopped the crawler just short of the column, which stretched for a full hundred meters across the light sand. "It won't take that long for them to go by, and enough of them die as it is without us running them down. I'll take a life when necessary, but not when there's a reasonable alternative."

They waited for almost half an hour, then moved on.

Pennington found a relatively sheltered spot that would protect them from the spritely night wind and they made camp just before nightfall, rushing to get the tent set up before full darkness, which came with surprising rapidity as the day ended. She prepared a hot meal, which was more welcome now. The day's heat vanished almost as quickly as the sunlight and the air was noticeably chill. McNabb found it uncomfortably quiet but Pennington could distinguish the myriad sounds of the night time desert, trollbugs grinding their pebbles, windsifters spreading their webs to catch flying insects, a tumithak digging itself a new underground corridor. Sometimes she thought she liked Ochre better at night than during the day, at least when she was in the desert.

In the past, Pennington had noticed that the people she guided tended to huddle closer together, both physically and mentally, when they found themselves separated from the rest of humanity. The two of them were three full days' travel from the nearest human settlement and tomorrow the gap would be even wider. But McNabb was proving to be an exception. He seemed impervious to loneliness, self contained, and unaltered by isolation. It was one of the few traits they shared and she wondered if she appeared as distant and self absorbed as he did.

While they were eating, McNabb launched into a monologue, explaining to Pennington why humanity would never have succumbed to the cultural failings that were widely believed to be the reason the natives of Ochre had become extinct, less than a thousand years before humans arrived on their world. Since McNabb had previously announced that the common wisdom about the fate of the Ochrans was just so much conjecture, McNabb's use of those same arguments to form his thesis this time struck Pennington as hypocritical. She listened just long enough to recognize that McNabb wasn't saying anything she hadn't heard before, then retreated into mimicry, pretending to be listening.

Eventually the man wound down and they went to sleep.

As usual, McNabb slept so late that Pennington became restless and went for a walk. He constantly complained that the trip was taking too long but didn't seem to feel any sense of urgency when his own convenience was involved. Pennington had realized by the end of the first day that he would pay her only the contracted amount, plus perhaps a token bonus, no matter how good a job she did, which effectively removed any incentive for her to exert herself on his behalf, so she let him sleep until he was ready to move on. This kind of penury didn't offend her particularly, since she was very careful about every credit she spent herself, but it didn't make her feel inclined to provide any extra consideration either.

Most of the people she'd previously guided through the desert had remarked on how desolate, featureless, and harsh it appeared, but Pennington saw beauty and variation where others saw ugliness and monotony. The content and density of the sand was constantly changing, there were fine gradations of color, and the infrequent breeze sometimes arranged the tiny dunes in surprisingly complex patterns. The water gatherers were all closely related because they were fashioned to accomplish the same tasks, but Pennington was able to distinguish among scores of variations, color, petal shape, surface texture, the angles at which the plants oriented themselves in relation to the ground and sun. And even the same landscape took on nuances at different times of day; light and shadow altered creating kaleidoscopic patterns, and the changing temperatures caused subtle adjustments in the petals of the water gatherers, curling or flattening them.

Pennington had long since given up trying to point out the beauty of Ochre's desert to her customers, particularly those like McNabb, who saw only what they wanted to see. She paused to watch thopter flies lighting on the leaves in search of minuscule droplets of dew, spotted a tractorpillar slowly making its way up the side of a gentle sand dune, and carefully avoided treading on a cluster of sand castles built by a colony of digger beetles. City dwellers thought the desert was mostly dead, but Pennington found it much livelier than any of the towns scattered across the fringelands. And a good deal more peaceful.

When she returned to the crawler, McNabb was awake, drinking kaffee. "How much further do we have to go?"

His expression dampened her mood. "And good morning to you too, McNabb. I told you before we left that it would take five to six days. If we keep at it, we can reach the ruins this evening some time, but we won't be able to make it there before dark. It would make more sense to camp at Howling Ridge and finish the trip in the morning."

McNabb made an impatient sound. "I'd rather push on and sleep behind solid walls."

"We're perfectly safe in the tent. The biggest predator around here is a kind of armored lizard the size of your foot, and they're not nocturnal and they don't like the way we smell. Or taste."

"I'm not frightened, Pennington. I'm just inconvenienced. I'd like to sleep in a real bed and piss into a recycler instead of the sand. And I have a lot of work to do once we arrive, and a limited time to finish it."

Pennington suppressed a flash of irritation. Had McNabb ever done field work before? She suspected not, or at least not any place that didn't have a three star hotel nearby. "Don't expect too much. Grogan Station will seem luxurious compared to what's waiting for us at the site. It's been abandoned for a long time, you know. There will be emergency supplies and beds, but don't expect luxury accommodations or haute cuisine."

McNabb grunted a response, grabbed his gear, and threw it into the back of the crawler. He was clearly annoyed at something. "We'll never get there at all if you don't move your ass." Pennington sighed and began to break camp.

Neither of them spoke for the next hour, which might have been uncomfortable if Pennington hadn't preferred the company of her own thoughts. But McNabb was irrepressible and eventually began to regale her with a list of the shortcomings and iniquities of the senior staff at the Collegium back on Marshak, occasionally breaking off for a critique of Concourse politics in general. The scenery began to change by mid-morning. An ancient volcano had scattered chunks of rock across this part of the desert, which looked like the board for some alien game of dice. Pennington could no longer follow a straight line toward their goal, was forced to weave back and forth, relying on instinct as much as memory. Sandstorms were comparatively gentle on Ochre, but they still managed to alter the landscape incrementally, and a route that was optimal last season might lead to a dead end today.

It was mid-afternoon before Howling Ridge appeared in the distance, shimmering in the heat. The jagged profile seemed almost artificial, but it was a natural phenomenon, a ridge of rock that had been cut into the shape of a raggedly serrated knife lying across the edge of the desert. Even a mild wind brought the ridge to life, generating oddly organic cries that sometimes made it difficult to sleep in close proximity. Pennington found the sounds soothing, but some of her clients had complained that it influenced their dreams, if they could sleep at all. She had tried to guess what McNabb's reaction would be, probably a conscious effort to appear unaffected, but now it seemed that they wouldn't be camping there and the crawler's engine would drown out all but the most penetrating external sounds as they passed.

They reached the ridge at dusk. Pennington worked their way along its length until she reached Lamentation Gate, the only breach in the barrier for twenty kilometers in either direction. It was the only sign of human activity the two men had seen all day because it was artificial, created to allow more direct surface traffic to the ruins. Drifting sand had partially obstructed the opening, but it was nothing the crawler couldn't handle and they passed through without incident.

The landscape was dramatically different on the west side of the ridge. Both flora and fauna were larger, more prolific, and more varied. There was even something that looked like a small tree with featherlike limbs and a porous, rubbery bark, and in the distance, falling under shadow now, the fringes of a genuine forest spilled down from the mountains beyond. The forests on Ochre were surprisingly earthlike and the dominant trees were very similar to conifers. The one startling difference was the complete lack of birds. No life form had developed the power of flight on Ochre for some reason, not even insects.

Pennington turned the crawler toward a shaded spot and shut down the engine.

"I thought we were going to drive straight through." There was a hint of anger in McNabb's voice, which Pennington decided to ignore.

"We are, unless you've changed your mind. But we won't get there before dark whatever we do and I need to stretch my legs and eat something more substantial than a ration cake." She stepped down from the cab without giving McNabb time to answer.

Howling Ridge wasn't living up to its name. There was a faint whistling moan but even that remained furtive and intermittent while Pennington prepared their meal. McNabb never helped, which was certainly his right since he had hired her services, but almost all of her previous clients had pitched in with the routine chores.

"What exactly are you planning to accomplish when we get there?" asked Pennington, despite her promise to herself not to inquire about the technical aspects of McNabb's one man expedition unless he chose to volunteer the information. "I thought the previous expeditions had pretty much exhausted the site. That's why it was abandoned." This was disingenuous of her. She had not been impressed with the abilities of the Blumenthal expeditions, both of which had included too high a proportion of novices and hangers on. The first had also been poorly equipped and both were ineptly managed, failings apparent even to a non-professional like herself. And she knew as well that the last group had been pulled out prematurely, in part because of the eruption of the Lysandran War and in part because they were underfunded. Or perhaps adequately funded if they hadn't spent so profligately.

"It was shoddy work. Blumenthal is lazy as well as biased. He tries to fit everything he finds into some universal theory of intelligence and tends to discard data which he can't reconcile. You remember what I told you about the consensus conclusion about the reason the Ochrans died out?"

Pennington nodded yes, but in truth she had tuned out most of McNabb's lectures on the subject. She searched her memory. "I know the accepted explanation is that they lost their purpose because there were no new frontiers to conquer. Which you think is nonsense."

McNabb nodded. "I think I used a more colloquial term. It's not even original with Blumenthal, but they've put his name on it because he's adopted the frontier thesis uncritically and imposes it on every culture he studies. The Ochrans did in fact explore and settle their world very quickly because, except for a handful of tiny islands, there's only this single land mass, immense though it may be. We're pretty sure they were ubiquitous as early as the hunter-gatherer stage of their cultural evolution. They had a single common language and we find evidence of uniformity everywhere. Ochrans in the colder regions wore less clothing than their cousins near the equator, but the styles were otherwise almost identical. They had very similar diets, social customs, burial procedures, and insofar as we understand it, a single religious system. You could pick up an Ochran at random and set him down anywhere else on the planet and he'd fit in effortlessly."

"But one day they just stopped breeding?"

"According to Blumenthal, that's exactly what happened, although since they were hermaphroditic, it would be more accurate to say they stopped conceiving. Not on one specific day, of course; not even Blumenthal's that stupid. But their population began to decline, slowly at first, more rapidly later. Tercalion and Burke have suggested that there might have been a physiological cause, a genetic defect that made them decreasingly fertile. It's possible, I suppose, but I don't endorse their theory myself, frankly, because the decline happened too quickly to be genetically determined. Blumenthal dismisses that possibility as well, one of his rare excursions into reasonable thought. After one of his usual superficial investigations Blumenthal decided that the Ochrans willed themselves to death because they lacked purpose in their lives." He made a disgusted sound and shook his head. "A racial suicide pact."

Pennington couldn't resist tweaking the other man. "Has anyone suggested a more plausible explanation? Blumenthal might be as bullheaded as you say, but that doesn't mean he's wrong."

McNabb threw his hands up in mock despair. "But it doesn't mean he's right either!" He closed his eyes, slowly lowered his arms. "Look, Pennington, where are you from originally?"

"I was born on Cascade, but that was a long time ago." And not just in years.

"What's the population of Cascade?"

Pennington shrugged. "I don't know, maybe fifty million. I haven't been back there in a long time."

"Doesn't matter. All right, out of that fifty million, how many will emigrate to another world?"

"How should I know?" Pennington thoughtshe could see where McNabb was going with this, but she had no intention of helping him arrive. "A few hundred? Maybe a thousand."

"I'd be surprised if it's that many. You see, Pennington, the vast majority of human beings have no desire at all to extend the frontier, to explore the unknown, to leave the safe and familiar. Admittedly, there is always a minority of restless people, most of them misfits, who keep moving away from the mass of humanity until there's no place further for them to go. They're not the glorious vanguard of our race; they're anomalies who serve a useful but limited purpose. Do you suppose that if the inhabitants of Cascade should someday discover that no one wanted to leave the planet any more that they would all quietly go home and stop making babies?"

Pennington could see the logic of his argument, even though she didn't entirely agree with its conclusion. And she wondered if he was including her among those "misfits" to which he had alluded. On the other hand, she supposed it wasn't an entirely unfair label. She'd always felt out of place on Cascade, and frequently felt the same way in Lachrymosia. It was only in the desert that she felt at ease. "I suppose not. So why do you think they're gone? The Ochrans, I mean."

"If I knew that, I wouldn't be wasting my time out here. But something in their environment must have changed. They had a stable, peaceful society. There's nothing indicating plague or famine or war or anything else catastrophic."

"Maybe races are like people. When they get too old, they start to decline. If nothing overt kills them, they just get tired of it all and grind to a halt."

"Nonsense!" McNabb clearly found the idea offensive. "Longevity never killed anyone. We're bound by the limits of the flesh not the mind."

"Don't I remember something about the suicide rate rising with the advent of longevity treatments?"

McNabb waved a hand to dismiss her argument. "That's not a valid analogy. You can't equate the actions of individuals to those of an entire race."

"But aren't races simply collections of individuals?"

He made a face that said she was a hopeless case and turned back to his food. Pennington felt she'd scored a point, even if her companion wouldn't acknowledge it.

"So what do you hope to find when we get there?" She gestured vaguely. "All the artifacts are gone, and everything has been recorded holographically. You could have completed your survey back in Port City without trekking all the way out here."

For the first time McNabb looked uncertain. "I've already done that. There's nothing in the recordings that explains what happened. They must have missed vital clues. And if I knew what I was looking for, I wouldn't have to look for it, would I? But I may have a clue." He fell suddenly silent, as though he'd said more than he'd intended. "Look, this is the largest and best preserved site on the planet. I want to walk around in it, get some idea of what it might have been like to live there, follow up on a couple of things Blumenthal overlooked."

"Teardrop has been stripped bare, McNabb. You'd be better off in Elegy or Farcry. Both of them have been preserved." Teardrop had been looted, as far as she was concerned.

"Restored in the image of Blumenthal's vision, you mean. They have potter shells scattered through the common areas even though we've always found them in alcoves and underground chambers. Whatever their purpose, it was private. They were not meant to be put on public display."

"It'd be a shame to hide them away. They're very pretty."

"But that's what the Ochrans did. That's just one of the questions for which we have no good answer."

Pennington said nothing. She agreed with McNabb that Blumenthal had done shoddy work, but she would never say so publicly. The Blumenthal Society steered clients her way from time to time and she had no desire to be blacklisted.

They finished their meal, packed up, and drove on into the darkness, four floodlights illuminating the way. There was little conversation during the balance of the trip, each of them lost in their own thoughts.

Pennington sensed the ruins before she actually saw them. She had spent a long time at Teardrop, having worked with the original survey that discovered them and throughout the extended period during which offworld investigators hoped that they would provide fresh insight into the Ochran culture. She had even met Blumenthal on a few occasions, and had found him to be tedious, irritable, and glib. He had been thorough in at least one regard; when his people finally pulled out of the site, they took everything with them that wasn't firmly fastened down. Despite its preserved state, Teardrop was too remote to turn into another showcase, so the artifacts had been harvested for display as part of a collection that bore Blumenthal's name.

As they crossed the last few kilometers, they were technically no longer in the desert, although there was still enough loose sand for the wind to shape into miniature dunes. The crawler could have crossed them without difficulty, but Pennington preferred not to risk getting even more sand in the engine compartment when it could be easily avoided. She turned and ran parallel to the dunes along a rib of granite, which was less direct, but McNabb wouldn't know the difference in the darkness.

The prefabricated buildings and pneumotents had all been taken away for reuse but one permanent cabin had been left intact for just such occasions as this. Solar panels on the roof accumulated the small power reserve required to operate the storage coolers and lighting and there was even a water tank and modern plumbing. Pennington was always careful not to abuse the system and always cleaned and aligned the collectors when she was at the site. McNabb wasn't the first client Pennington had brought to Teardrop since the site had been abandoned and probably would not be the last. Most stayed only a day or two, preferring to devote more attention to the sexier sites elsewhere, and the increasingly rare tourist never spent more than a single night after seeing the desolate, despoiled ruins. There was a semi-enclosed shelter adjacent to the cabin and the crawler fit inside easily. Pennington killed the engine and all but one of the external lights.

"Home at last," she said to her companion, but McNabb had already opened the door on his side and was stepping down.

The cabin wasn't locked and probably hadn't been visited since Pennington's last trip out. She wasn't the only guide working this part of Ochre, but no one else appreciated the desert as she did, and they were usually more than happy to leave her that portion of their clientele, preferring to spend their time taking botanists and the occasional tourist through the lush coastal regions, although if business didn't pick up soon they'd be less fastidious in the future.

The interior lights came on as soon as they entered. Pennington took a quick look around and ascertained that everything appeared to be in order. The storage area's telltales were all green and the double row of bunks was undisturbed. A lattice weaver had managed to get in somehow and its intricate web filled one corner near the ceiling, but there was no other indication of a breach.

"I want to get an early start in the morning." McNabb was already sitting on a bunk, examining the pillow critically.

Pennington smiled to herself, knowing how unlikely that was. "Whatever you say. Let's get the rest of the gear inside."

Although Pennington was up well before McNabb the following morning she had to admit that it wasn't as long a wait as it had been in the past. She had already finished a quick walk through of the nearest cluster of dome shaped buildings, just to make sure there weren't any surprises waiting for them. On one trip, a client had stepped into a newly dug paraviper pit, and while the tiny serpent's venom wouldn't have done any harm even if it had been able to penetrate the woman's boot, she did twist her ankle badly on her very first day, and she'd expressed her displeasure at length as she hobbled around thereafter.

McNabb had explored the holographic mockup of Teardrop back at the institute in Lachrymosia, so theoretically he knew his way around the ruins without assistance. The reality and a copy, no matter how accurate, are two entirely different things, and Pennington could tell that the man became disoriented more than once during the course of the morning, although he never asked for help. The guide occupied herself cleaning out the engine compartment again and they didn't actually have a conversation until the mid-day meal.

"So tell me again what you're hoping to accomplish here."

McNabb sighed, but his heart wasn't in it. He was positively ebullient for the first time since they'd met. "Not to put too fine a point on it, I wish to prove Blumenthal wrong. No, that's not quite right. Most of his conclusions are almost certainly correct. I wish to prove him superficial and sloppy."

"If he has as many enemies as you claim, I'm surprised you're not heading a full expedition."

"By rights, I should be, and believe me, there are a lot of people who hope I'm successful, although few will own up to it.

Blumenthal isn't admired so much as feared. He wields a lot of power, and not just within my field. A smile or a frown from him can determine the distribution of grants and budgets across a broad range of disciplines."

"So how do you go about that? Proving his shortcomings, I mean."

"Well, that's a bit technical. I assume you're reasonably familiar with what we know, or think we know, about the Ochrans?"

"Reasonably, yes. I know that they didn't leave a lot of written records behind, and that we've never found an intact body. They probably lived a lot longer than we did and their population grew very slowly, though we don't know whether that was by choice or through some physical restriction on reproduction."

"These factors deprive us of our two best clues as to their nature," interrupted McNabb. "We've reconstructed what they must have looked like from various surviving fragments, and from drawings. They never developed photography, unfortunately."

She had seen various renditions of the Ochrans, which varied only in fine detail. "They looked like oversized beetles pretending to be human."

"I wouldn't characterize it that way, but essentially you're correct. They were four-limbed and walked upright with bodies enclosed in shell, overlapping plates of reinforced cartilage actually. We know they were on average a little shorter than we are, and rather broader, but not grotesquely so. And there was an internal skeleton to which the shell plates were attached by a series of thick muscles. At least we think that's true, based on irregularities on the bones that probably served as anchor points."

"I know that no one has ever found a graveyard of any kind. Did their bodies just rot away?"

McNabb shook his head. "The fragments that remain are quite resilient. No, we're certain now that they deliberately disposed of their dead, for either sanitary or religious reasons no doubt. Most likely they're buried but we've never found any proof of that. Blumenthal suggests they were taken out to sea and cast off, but that seems unlikely. There's no evidence that they visited the off shore islands, for example, and they built roads parallel to rivers instead of using the rivers themselves. We've never found anything suggesting that they traveled on the water, and an analysis of bones in their refuse pits suggests that they didn't even eat fish."

"There are no real fish on Ochre."

"The equivalent lifeforms then," he said shortly. "Their coastal and riverfront communities were no larger than those totally landlocked. I'm not sure they had an aversion to the water, but they were at least indifferent to it."

"If Blumenthal was right, maybe they avoided the water because it was the abode of the dead."

"Nonsense!"

"Well, if there are no graveyards, where are their bones? There are plenty of carrion eaters on Ochre, but I've never seen one that could chew up hardened bone."

"This is only conjecture, mind you, but there's some evidence that they routinely destroyed the bodies of the dead, literally ground the bones to powder. It may have been a religious ritual, mixing the dust of the body with the soil of the planet, or casting it into the wind to be carried away to some other plane of existence. Or they may have used it in some form or ritual cannibalism. We have as yet no clue to their motives."

"Aren't the potter shells supposed to have some religious significance?"

Potter shells were one of the ongoing mysteries of Ochre. They were fairly common because every Ochran residence ever found had one or more of them tucked away in its "basement,", although not one of them had ever been found elsewhere. Their origin and purpose remained mysteries. Although they resembled pottery, they were obviously organically derived, convoluted, gourd-like objects of varying sizes and colorations, hollow, and with a highly polished exterior. Initially they were believed to be the shells of some marine lifeform like the nautilus of old Earth, but they had all been scraped clean and evidently scoured internally before being placed in storage, rendering them virtually useless to xenobiologists. Nothing remotely similar had been found living in Ochre's small surviving oceans, or anywhere else on the planet.

McNabb was nodding. "The evidence points that way, but it's complicated. There are also good reasons to believe that they were indicators of social status, and that they changed hands from time to time, perhaps functioning as a form of currency."

155

"They sure took a lot of them out of here." Pennington remembered the caravan of commercial crawlers that had carted off literally thousands of the potter shells, along with everything else portable.

McNabb's face darkened. "Yes, and without proper documentation. They recorded the first few chambers, but after that they just carted the shells away as quickly as they found them. It apparently never occurred to anyone that the arrangement of the shells within a particular storage area might be significant. I've examined the few cases handled more professionally and I've detected recurring patterns, but with such a small amount of data, it's impossible to do more than speculate."

The food was gone and Pennington began cleaning up. She had dug a waste pit behind the cabin. Before they left, she would incinerate all of its contents and cover the ashes. McNabb watched without offering to help and Pennington was surprised to find him still sitting at their makeshift dining table, a mostly level slab of rock, when she returned. McNabb seemed to be lost in his own thoughts and Pennington hesitated, not certain whether or not she should speak. But after a few seconds, McNabb turned toward her.

"Come with me a minute. I want to show you something."

It took more than a minute. The ruins looked a little bit like an adobe village, or would have if there had been more straight lines. There was evidence that the solidly built buildings, ranging from a single story to three high, had been brightly decorated when they were occupied, but by now they'd all been reduced to an anonymous, buff color, their rare sharp edges rounded, the exposed surfaces burnished smooth by wind and rain and blowing sand. Only one or two of them had suffered significant damage, plus one entire block that had succumbed to a landslide during the year after Teardrop had been first discovered. There had been an outcry at the time that the damage was the result of the excavation, but in fact it occurred in an area that had barely been touched. Ochre was pretty active tectonically, and every year saw a handful of quakes strong enough to rattle nerves and cause minor damage. Pennington took them in stride. Out in the desert, there usually wasn't anything that could fall on you and she'd only once seen an open fissure, and it was narrow enough that she stepped across it.

The Ochrans, whose bodies and limbs were assembled from arcs and spheres rather than straight lines, generally eschewed the direct in their architecture as well. The walls all leaned very slightly inward, so that ceilings were always smaller than the floors, and the perimeters of most of their buildings were discernibly oval. Their streets were actually footpaths, since they had no vehicles larger than pushcarts and no draft animals to pull wagons and their intersections were mostly merges rather than crossings. These pathways meandered among the buildings, gradually rising as the city had grown too large for its original site and had expanded up the increasingly steep slope into the mountains.

Pennington prided herself on staying in good physical condition, so she was surprised to find herself straining to keep up with the older man, and relieved when he finally reached a small plateau and came to a stop. "This is the second oldest Ochran city we've discovered, and most of Elegia is underwater."

"So I understand." Pennington's side ached slightly and she was breathing hard. She was also sweating even though it was noticeably cooler on this side of Howling Ridge. Too much sitting around between jobs, she told herself. And she wasn't getting any younger either. "It's a shame they died off before they had time to develop a real technology. They might have been interesting neighbors."

McNabb shook his head. "The Ochrans weren't a young race. Their civilization was stable for longer than the entire span of human history to date. Unfortunately, nature stacked the deck against them. There are few minerals near the surface, so mining would have required an extraordinary effort. Their diets were predominantly vegetarian, at least so we believe, because we've found ample proof of their agricultural expertise but no sign at all of animal husbandry. There are, as you have noted, no serious competitors, only scavengers, small predators, and numerous prey."

"They couldn't have evolved in a vacuum. And they were pretty rugged under all that sheathing."

"Nor did they. Those fossilized bones we saw out in the desert prove that. We can only assume that they consciously eliminated all of the higher animals. The only other potential competition was factions within their own race, but as far as we can tell, they never developed the artificial divisions that have troubled our own past. Either that or they eliminated the nonconformers quickly. They had no nations, no central government, even though their commercial enterprises were quite complex. There was regular trade from every region of the planet, even the poles. We have yet to find evidence of a tribal system or regional rivalries and frankly I don't think we ever will. They were marvelously cooperative, but there was no stimulus to evolve as a culture."

"So eventually they lost the will to live and just pined away?" Pennington deliberately prodded her companion.

"Of course not!" McNabb was visibly insulted. "They were probably quite happy with the status quo. Remember those millions of your neighbors back on Cascade, the ones who have no interest in ever leaving. That's what the Ochrans were like. And for them, there was no place to go in any case. Remember, this is the planet's only landmass, and there's not even a moon to tantalize them."

McNabb had apparently gotten his second wind, because he straightened up and beckoned. "This way. It's not far now."

Pennington hadn't been up this particular path in a long time. During her previous visits, she'd been kept busy by her employers, preparing meals, running errands, helping with mapping or measurements. She had been all over the site, but hadn't always had the leisure to really examine her surroundings.

Although most of their structures were free standing, the Ochrans had built several dwellings right into the face of the mountain and had modified a large shelf of rock into a kind of courtyard – probably a marketplace or whatever passed for a social center. Further expansion in this direction had apparently come to a halt when they broke into a natural cave system, a fairly extensive one that led down into the interior of the mountain. It was in fact a not quite extinct volcano, and the caves were riddled with steam vents and the occasional sulfurous plume, both of which could be quite dangerous. A few tentative efforts had been made to explore the caves, but there was no evidence that the Ochrans had ever made use of them. They had in fact blocked all but one of the entrances and that one was so well concealed that it hadn't even been found until the second expedition.

But that was where McNabb was leading them.

"Hold it! Do you really want to go in there?" She felt both an almost visceral apprehension and a more reasoned reluctance to enter without the proper equipment and someone to stand by outside in case of an emergency. "It's dark in there and we don't have lights with us."

They had negotiated a rather treacherous path, narrow and badly eroded, with the wall of a large building, probably a granary, on their left and a precipitous drop into a ragged cleft in the mountainside on their right. Now they faced an entrance cut like a slit in the rock face directly ahead.

"There are vents above us and I have a flasher. We can't go far without bringing better lights, but we should be all right in the first chamber. Come on. We won't go far."

Pennington suspected that McNabb's invitation had been motivated by his unwillingness to enter the caves alone rather than a genuine wish to share the experience. Although she disliked being manipulated and considered refusing for safety reasons, she'd expended too much effort climbing this far to back out without appearing childish. And truthfully, she was rather curious. She'd never been inside the cave during any of her previous visits to Teardrop.

Curiosity notwithstanding, she almost turned back a few minutes later and would have done so except that McNabb forged forward relentlessly and apparently fearlessly. The passageway wove back and forth in such an exaggerated fashion that they were in total darkness almost from the outset, other than the beam from McNabb's flasher. Pennington found herself wondering how such a regular tunnel could have been created naturally, then realized her error. It was obviously artificial, which suggested that Blumenthal and others had made a serious error in dismissing the caves as irrelevant. They were in part at least an artifact, not a natural formation. But if the Ochrans had built or at least redesigned hem, why create such an indirect route? It was as though they had wanted to discourage entry, but if that was the case, why not cover the entrance over as completely as they had the other openings?

The cone of moving light she'd been following disappeared suddenly and she halted and called out. A second passed, then McNabb became slightly visible ahead, an outline more than a shape, then a shadow, then an actual body. "Come on. It's not much further." He waved the flasher and she glimpsed smooth surfaced walls and a ceiling far above her head. The passageway was much larger here than near the surface.

They emerged into a surprisingly large cavern which seemed startlingly bright at first, but only because they had been in near complete darkness. Once they adjusted, they realized that the illumination came from three widely spaced openings in the outside wall. McNabb turned off his flasher and they could still see reasonably clearly.

"Those vents aren't natural," said Pennington, unnecessarily. The openings were all very close to perfect circles, or would have been if vines hadn't grown over the edges, dropping leafy tentacles into the gloom. They could hear running water somewhere in the distance and, briefly, the hiss of a steam vent relieving itself. A spongy, grayish moss covered large portions of the walls, the rest appeared bare. Something small but furtive moved in the distance, its claws clicking on the stone floor.

"Blumenthal decided that the cave was anomalous and therefore not worth investigating. The Ochrans obviously came here, but they left no artifacts behind. None that have been found anyway. If this place held some significance for them, the reasons might be lost forever. His philosophy has always been not to waste time on problems that have no obvious solution so predictably he redirected his resources elsewhere."

"Sounds practical."

McNabb made a disgusted sound. "Blumenthal is always practical, but he's not always smart. The very fact that this place is anomalous makes it more significant, not less so." His voice altered slightly, shedding some of its self confidence. "At least that's my hope. All of the exploration in here has been cursory at best, and they never even finished mapping it. There are vast sub-chambers and miles of tunnels that weren't even entered."

It occurred to Pennington that even if there was something significant to find in the caves, it could take months to explore them adequately, even with a fully outfitted team. "I think you're gambling against very high odds. Are you planning just to wander around looking for an Ochran signpost that Blumenthal's people missed? Do you really expect to just stumble onto something significant given the short time we have here?"

He shook his head. "I'm convinced that these caves have something more to tell us, and something important. The Ochrans wouldn't have taken such pains to make them hard to enter if there wasn't a good reason for discouraging visitors. And there were hints in the recordings made by Blumenthal's people that they held some particular significance for the Ochrans."

Pennington reflected for a moment. "Okay, let's say I agree with you that there is some mystery involved here that Blumenthal missed. How are you going to find what he overlooked, working alone and with limited time? Like you said, they didn't leave anything behind to help us."

"Ah, that's not exactly what I said. The Ochrans didn't leave anything in here, at least not that we've ever found. But I did find a reference to this place in the recordings of one of the buildings down below."

Pennington's curiosity increased despite her antipathy. "What kind of reference?"

McNabb smiled and remained silent for a few seconds, relishing his moment. "I found a map, or part of one anyway. Whoever did the recording of this particular building was sloppy. It's carved into a wall and only a fragment of it is was holographed. Criminal negligence and further proof that proper research must be conducted in situ."

"What kind of a map?"

"As I said, it was inscribed on an interior wall of one the largest buildings. Blumenthal has it marked as possibly a form of non-representational art. Even if he was right, that would have made it a major find. Everything we know of the Ochrans tells us that they were less than imaginative in any abstract sense."

Pennington remained skeptical. "Are you telling me that no one else has made the connection? How is that possible?"

"With Blumenthal, overlooking things is probable not just possible. For one thing, they had already abandoned exploration of the cave when they found the map, and the team who worked that building had never been inside the mountain. But even if they had, they might not have realized its significance. I almost missed it myself. Look at this." He removed his datapad from a pocket and activated the holoscreen. "Here's a reproduction of the map."

Pennington examined the shimmering image, which seemed to consist solely of an amorphous shape with attenuated edges. "That's a map of the caves? I don't see it. The main chamber is roughly circular. This is a rhomboid."

McNabb smiled secretively and touched an icon. A second image hovered over the first, a malformed circle with frayed edges. "That's the entrance there, see?"

Pennington squinted and nodded. "That looks more like it."

"Now watch." He reduced the second image to a tenth its size, then moved it across the face of the first until it neatly superimposed itself over one small excrescence.

"Damn!" said Pennington. McNabb had something after all. "How far do the caves extend then?"

"Down into the heart of the mountain, I'd guess," said McNabb gleefully. "Perhaps even to the opposite side. And Blumenthal's people never went to look."

She peered at the datascreen. "None of that shows on your map."

"Of course not, because the fools didn't record the rest of it. All we have to do is find the right building and record the rest."

She sighed. "There are over five thousand intact structures, McNabb. That's a lot of places to look."

"Then we'd better get started."

It took two days to find the right chamber and it was Pennington who found the elongated oval room with what appeared to be a mural covering the walls. McNabb was as close to sociable as she'd ever seen him as he carefully recorded every detail, uploading it into his datapad. Pennington could see why it had been dismissed as decorative. It seemed much too large and complex to be a map of any real location, an elaborate maze whose passages looped back on one another, sometimes intersecting, sometimes passing over or under other sections. There were a few blank spots where, she assumed, solid rock blocked potential routes, and there were a few recurring symbols, one resembling a stylized flame which she suspected – correctly as it turned out – indicated the presence of steam vents.

"They must have spent generations digging these tunnels," she observed. "Even with automated equipment it would have taken years. Why go to so much effort?"

McNabb shrugged. "Why build the Pyramids? They had no practical value, after all."

"Do you think that's what this is? A gigantic tomb for one of their leaders?" She knew that was wrong the moment she spoke. "Or a mass tomb. This could be where they brought their dead."

McNabb smiled broadly. "That's my theory. And if I'm right, there must be similar facilities near their other population centers. Some of them must have survived, but we haven't found them yet."

The recording was finished and McNabb began processing the imagery on his datapad. "This won't take long. Then we can start exploring the caves more systematically."

"Not today we won't. It'll be dark soon."

McNabb glanced at her and frowned. "In the morning then, first thing."

"Whenever you say." She still didn't like the idea of the two of them entering the caves without a safety watch outside, but McNabb's excitement was infectious. And they had a map. They wouldn't get lost.

McNabb spent the evening bent over his datapad. He had identified three features of paramount interest, two oval chambers too regular to be natural, and a third that was so nearly perfectly circular that it had obviously been excavated. He charted a course that would pass through one of the ovals and terminate at the circle. The second oval was much further, almost at the opposite side of the mountain range.

The previous expedition had assigned numerical designations to the handful of tunnels and chambers they had examined to serve as a rudimentary guide, but they had never installed extensive lighting and whatever they had deployed had been taken away when they pulled up stakes. McNabb and Pennington would have to deal with the same problem. McNabb might have been willing to proceed with only the shoulder lights on his biosuit and a flasher, but Pennington refused to consider taking that great a risk, particularly after McNabb admitted having included a couple of hundred lightweight glowpads in his equipage.

"All right, I suppose it's better to be safe. We'll bring the glowpads and the rest of the equipment up tomorrow and extend our work radius systematically."

It proved to be easier said than done. The crawler was too big for the comparatively narrow streets so they were forced to carry everything by hand up a gentle but very long slope. They were both exhausted by the time they had finished their second trip, storing everything just inside the cave entrance. "I suppose we could carry up bedding and food as well and sleep in here."

Pennington shook her head. "Too claustrophobic for me. And I'll bet this place is full of creepy crawlies when the light goes." She pointed to the mossy walls. "That's stickymoss. Those fronds are coated with adhesive. When anything small enough to get caught crosses them, the moss has lunch. With this much moss around," she made a sweeping gesture with both arms, "there must be a healthy food supply."

McNabb didn't argue the point, was apparently perfectly happy to have a reason for not sleeping in the cavern. "Maybe one of the Ochran buildings then. We could secure the entrance to discourage scavengers." There was a colony of whizzers somewhere near their base camp and they had to be careful about leaving small objects around where the mischievous and very fast creatures could spirit them away to their burrows.

"We'd have to live on ration packs up here. No cooking facilities. No refrigeration. I'd rather walk back down and have a warm meal once a day."

"You're probably right. I just wish it didn't take so long to go back and forth."

That reminded Pennington, who checked the time. "We'd better start back. I don't relish making that cliff walk in the dark."

The following day was physically wearing, at least for Pennington. They carried a substantial load of equipment on their first trip, establishing a storage area just beyond the last dogleg of the convoluted cavern entrance. Pennington had suggested using the closest of the intact buildings outside the cave, but McNabb vetoed it. "I don't want to have to make my way back and forth through that damned entrance every time I need something."

Pennington was sent off to fetch more equipment while McNabb began affixing the glowpads to the cave walls, extending the area of illumination deeper into the mountain. The wafer thin lighting stuck readily enough to the walls and cast a soft light that emphasized rather than eliminated the shadows, but it would make walking back and forth over the uneven surfaces considerably safer. They dimmed automatically when outside the range of the transmitter in McNabb's suit and their stored power should last much longer than would be necessary.

One of the marked tunnels had collapsed and a second was almost impassable because of a steam vent which had apparently not existed when the map was drawn, but by the end of that day, the lighted area had multiplied tenfold and McNabb had identified an acceptable alternate route to bypass the obstructions. By the second day, they had already been in chambers never before visited by human beings. Pennington carried a spare transmitter in her belt pouch so there was no longer any necessity for them to remain together, although she was uneasy whenever McNabb insisted that they separate.

They were together when they reached the oval chamber early on the third day. Pennington found it very disappointing. There were some glyphs inscribed on the walls but as yet no one could read Ochran – assuming these were words of some kind and not just decorative. McNabb scored a minor victory when he found an Ochran artifact, the broken handle of some implement, lying in one corner.

"Possibly a torch or lantern," he told Pennington. "They had no other form of artificial light that we've been able to identify, not even oil lamps."

"That's a long way to carry a torch. And presumably they had to come back the same way."

"I doubt they used the torches until they arrived at their destination." He smiled at Pennington's look of confusion. "Once they had a passageway charted, they could probably negotiate it in the dark and save the torches for use only when necessary. I believe they had remarkable memories, perhaps eidetic, which may explain the scarcity of written records. They didn't need them."

Pennington considered the prospect of wandering through these tunnels in absolute darkness, one arm out to feel for the wall perhaps, and shivered with revulsion. "That would take considerable determination."

"You're making the same mistake Blumenthal did. He interprets everything from a human viewpoint. For all we know, the Ochrans weren't bothered by absolute darkness. They might even have been able to generate some form of bioluminescence. Remember, they were alien. We don't know how their minds worked, or their bodies."

"At times I don't even understand how human minds work, let alone alien ones. Point taken."

They continued to affix glowpads at strategic points for the rest of that day, gradually extending their area of operation deeper into the mountain. Trips back to the storage area now consumed almost as much time as the climb from base camp to the entrance. Pennington wondered how long it would be before the last of the glowpads was in place and if they had enough to reach the circular chamber that was McNabb's ultimate goal. Over breakfast the following morning, she raised the possibility of a shortfall.

"I brought two hundred of them with me, and we can space them further apart if we run short. If absolutely necessary we can do the last leg of the trip without them. I've come too far to go away empty handed."

Five days passed before McNabb began to grow discouraged, or at least let Pennington sense his mood. Half of the glowpads were in place and they had penetrated as much as a full mile into the mountain. That still left another mile to their goal and time was becoming more of a factor. They had provisions with them for thirty days, and there were flashfrozen emergency rations stored – considerably less appetizing – in the cabin which might last as long again. Pennington was curious enough to stay on a day or two past her contract without pay, but no longer than that, and McNabb avoided the subject when she brought it up. She suspected he was topped out and had no credit left that he was able, or at least willing, to spend.

Given that McNabb was underfunded, an extended stay was problematic. If they used the supplies stored at the cabin, they would be expected to pay for their replenishment. Alternatively, they could radio for a supply drop, which McNabb almost certainly could not afford. He raised the possibility that Pennington might go on a supply run by herself while he continued to work at the site, but she wouldn't even consider it.

"I won't leave you alone out here overnight let alone for the length of time it would take to get to the nearest settlement. I'd lose my license even if nothing happened to you."

Food wasn't Pennington's only concern. On the fifth day, she had found McNabb treating a burn on his arm from the medikit and demanded an explanation.

"I was passing a steam vent and I lost my footing and got scalded. It's not serious." Pennington insisted on examining the wound, which was in fact relatively minor, but it suggested the possibility of further and more worrying injuries. Pennington decided to stay closer to her client on the following day's exploration, and followed McNabb into a portion of the cave system that was stifling hot and humid even though it was not near any visible steam vents. It also smelled strongly of sulfur and other gases. Breathing it irritated their sinuses and their eyes watered constantly.

"I don't think this is a good place to be. Why don't we try one of the other passages?"

"They're too roundabout. As you keep telling me, we don't have an infinite amount of time." McNabb sounded petulant.

"If one or both of us collapse because of poisonous fumes, get parboiled by a steam vent, or fall into one of the chasms, all the time in the world won't help."

McNabb would not be deterred from the plans he'd made. He had found a second abandoned torch nearby, this one intact, and was convinced that this was the preferred path of the Ochrans. "If there's anything to find along the way, this is where it will be." Pennington wasn't mollified and decided they could no longer afford the risk of operating independently, even though she was not thrilled with the thought of spending even more time in McNabb's company. She was also freshly cognizant of the dangers they faced. If they became incapacitated down here, they could die very quickly, either boiled alive by an erupting steam vent or asphyxiated by toxic gas, or very slowly, trapped or injured and with no one likely to look for them for at least a few weeks. There were breathing masks in the crawler, but they only functioned for short periods if disconnected from the air sparger. She retrieved them even though they really weren't adequate for the conditions they faced and insisted they carry them. McNabb agreed grudgingly. Pennington made no effort to conceal her irritation. If McNabb had warned her that they'd be working underground, she would have planned accordingly and borrowed a pair of rebreathers.

On the ninth day, it was Pennington rather than McNabb who first noticed the markings. According to the map they were very close to their goal, would reach it before day's end unless they encountered some unexpected delay. They had both been concentrating on their footing because the route was flanked on both sides by active steam vents. It was possible, barely, to walk between them without getting burned, arms pressed tightly against their sides, legs together so that they were forced to take small, mincing steps. Pennington wondered how the Ochrans, whose bodies were considerably broader than humans, had managed to negotiate this particular passage without getting singed around the edges.

McNabb had his head down because an inch or more of loose sand meant footing was treacherous as well. Pennington paused to catch her breath, let her eyes trail up the far wall, and in the peripheral glow from McNabb's shoulder lights she saw that the stone had been carved to display a single symbol, a twisted sphere whose shape she recognized immediately.

Despite her weariness and the steady dissipation of her initial enthusiasm, she felt a rush of excitement. "McNabb! Look up ahead!"

McNabb stopped and raised his arm carefully to play his flasher around the cavern. Shadows were chased from a darker recess, revealing the entrance to another narrow tunnel, this one so symmetrically cut that it was clearly artificial. Above the entrance, someone had carved from sheer stone a very accurate rendition of one of the potter shells that the Ochrans hoarded beneath their homes. McNabb consulted his datapad. "We're close," he said unnecessarily.

"What do you suppose that means?" She played her own flasher around the walls but there were no other symbols that she could see.

"This must be the entrance to their whatever it is, some kind of sacred place." McNabb started forward hastily, remembered his situation at the last moment and avoided what could have been a painful reminder. The steam vent to their right doubled in intensity for a few seconds, as though to bar the way, then died back to near quiet. The one to their left hadn't so much as hiccoughed since they'd arrived, a plume of heat and sound so great that they were forced to shout to make themselves heard. The muted glow made shadows writhe on the walls.

They continued methodically across the dangerous stretch and reached the relative safety of the farther passageway without mishap, but McNabb's rekindled enthusiasm took a bad hit when they passed through the archway. Just beyond, a tumbled pile of rock blocked their way.

It took two full days to clear enough of the obstruction to create a negotiable path through the rubble, and even then they only succeeded because Pennington rigged one of her spare powercells to overload and split the rock into several more manageable chunks. The contained explosion shattered the massive boulder they'd been unable to shift by hand, but it had also precipitated a landslide that almost dropped them both into a steam vent. When the ground, and the two interlopers, had all stopped shaking, the passage was still blocked, but by rubble rather than a single immovable mass. They had been able to clear it by throwing or rolling the fragments into the chasm behind them.

. McNabb chafed at every delay, however slight, and seriously proposed that they spend the night underground. Pennington patiently explained, and not for the first time, that it was too dangerous, that they could be overcome by fumes while they slept and never waken. They argued, McNabb threatened to fire the guide, and Pennington responded with a threat of her own. If she used her radio to report a dangerously uncooperative client, an enforcement skimmer would be sent out to bring them both back. McNabb could be fined and expelled from Ochra if Pennington's account convinced the adjudicator that he had been acting irresponsibly. Of course the converse was that if they found in McNabb's favor, she'd face a crippling fine, suspension or revocation of her license, and would effectively be out of business. Fortunately, McNabb yielded, though quite ungraciously and wouldn't speak to her again until the next morning.

It was late afternoon of the following day when they finally broke through the final obstruction, mostly loose shale. Ordinarily Pennington would have insisted that further exploration wait until they were both rested and re-equipped, but she knew it would be impossible to restrain McNabb and she was in fact rather curious herself to know what lay ahead. So she scrambled forward in his wake, cautioning McNabb to move slowly and carefully until they could judge the terrain ahead.

The collapse had only affected a relatively small portion of the tunnel, after which they could walk normally. The passageway was almost completely clear of litter, the floor so clean in places that it might have been swept. The walls receded far enough that they could have progressed side by side and although there was a trace of sourness in the air, there were no steam vents and the temperature was perceptibly dropping. McNabb wasn't bothering to affix glowpads to the walls and was relying entirely on his shoulder lights and flasher, moving steadily forward. Pennington opened her mouth to say something, then thought better of it.

They emerged into a huge cave, the biggest they'd encountered so far, an undefined blob on the map was the last major feature before they reached the circular chamber. The tunnel opened onto a broad natural shelf of rock beyond which the floor fell away into darkness so deep that they couldn't see the bottom even when they leaned over to let their lights shine down. A similar though narrower shelf was visible at the opposite side of the cavern and at first it seemed that there was no way to get across.

"There must have been a bridge at one time," suggested Pennington, but McNabb shook his head.

"There's nothing to indicate that, either here or on the map. There has to be a way across. They couldn't fly."

In the end it was Pennington who solved the problem, although she later regretted the impulse that made her point out the way across. They would have been far better off returning to the surface for a meal and a night's sleep. But after scanning their surroundings with her lights, she raised her arm and shouted to McNabb, who turned and, after a moment, recognized what she had found. The irregular line inscribed along the far wall was in fact a very narrow ledge that extended into a shadowy alcove to their right, then continued on the near side of the abyss, terminating at a point accessible to them if they scrambled up a steep slope of crumbling rock.

"They didn't make it easy, did they?" asked Pennington.

"It probably wasn't this formidable when they were using it. A lot of things change in a thousand years."

There was no stopping McNabb now, and Pennington didn't even try, though she did remind him to be cautious.

The lengthy crossing left both of them shaken. The ledge was so narrow in places that Pennington couldn't understand how the Ochrans, whose bodies were much wider, managed it at all. It had probably been wider originally. The edges were crumbling and more than once she caught her breath as a piece of rock turned under her foot and fell into the darkness. Another thousand years of erosion and it wouldn't be passable for anything but cave lizards and insects. It climbed and dropped constantly, and the grainy rock and sand was slippery and deceptive. Somehow they reached the opposite side, where they collapsed for a time, their nerves taut and their calf muscles tight and painful. Pennington thought she might just sit where she was and let McNabb go the rest of the way on his own, but when he stood up again and began moving she sighed, rose, and followed.

They reached another tunnel, probably natural in origin although it had clearly been intentionally widened. The walls were curved and sloping in the Ochran fashion, and they had been polished smooth, as had the floor and ceiling. A light layer of dust and fine sand lay on the floor, but it was otherwise just as it had been when the Ochrans were still alive. "It's just ahead," said McNabb in a husky whisper.

They advanced another forty paces and found themselves at last in the final chamber. McNabb shifted his body so that his lights swept the area and then gasped and gave a nervous laugh. "At last! I was beginning to wonder if I'd ever find it."

In the center of the chamber stood a pedestal carved of stone, and on top of the pedestal were about a dozen potter shells. Pennington was reminded of the altar in the church her parents had made her attend back on Cascade. She felt a rush of uneasiness, as if she'd been caught performing some grotesquely profane act. McNabb obviously felt no such inhibition.

He strode directly to the pedestal and stood staring down at the shells, not touching them, as though he was afraid that they were part of an elaborate illusion and that they would disappear if he broke the spell. Pennington was less absorbed and she directed her lights around the perimeter of the room, because it was clearly designed to be a room and not just a cave.

At one end stood several rows of wooden cages. They looked very much like the human equivalent except that the corners were rounded in the usual Ochran fashion, showing their disdain for straight lines. They were constructed from a kind of wicker with a very fine mesh. Most of the cages were withered and worn; jagged splits had in some cases widened to yawning gaps, and a few had collapsed into complete ruin. The desiccated air had helped preserve them and their general purpose was obvious. But what had they held captive? They were far too small to house Ochran criminals, if the Ochrans even had criminals.

"McNabb, come look at this." She turned. McNabb had moved away from the altar. He was standing at the opposite side of the room, staring down at something on the floor. Pennington called him again, but there was still no reaction. Curious, she made her way around the pedestal, her lights sweeping ahead. And then she saw what held McNabb's attention.

On the floor lay the intact remains of an adult Ochran, the first ever found.

It was only a skeleton, of course, along with the outer shell plates, the latter detached and disordered. The leathery skin was gone, as were the internal organs, but all of the hard structures remained and as far as Pennington could tell, they were undamaged. There was nothing to indicate the cause of death – poisonous gas, old age, a stab wound, a disease, or whatever. It was lying on its side, one leg tucked up, the other out straight, the arms held close to the torso. If the Ochran had curled up and gone to sleep and never wakened, it would have looked much the same. Perhaps that was exactly what had happened.

"This alone justifies this trip," said McNabb hoarsely. "Coupled with the elaborate nature of this chamber and the pedestal, I think Blumenthal is going to have to revisit his theories. Obviously the Ochrans weren't quite as informal and ritual free as he would like us to think." He sounded immensely satisfied with himself.

Pennington crouched and examined the remains. "It looks like he or she was holding one of the potter shells when he died." She pointed toward a recognizably shaped object lying partly concealed beneath the chest cavity.

McNabb joined her, staring silently for a while, then gave a visible start. "I'll be damned!"

Pennington blinked. "What is it?"

"That shell. It's not under the body. It's inside it."

Pennington looked again, more closely this time, and frowned. "I don't understand." But that wasn't entirely true. She was beginning to understand exactly what that might mean.

"The shells. They aren't some kind of sea creature. They're an internal structure of the Ochrans themselves. An armored chamber, probably for their heart, or its equivalent. No wonder they treated them as religious objects. Those are the hearts, the symbolic souls perhaps, of their ancestors. Pennington, this is going to change everything we know – or think we know - about them. And it probably even explains why they destroyed the bodies of the dead. They did it to remove the heart cavity and move it to a place of honor. I never suspected anything like this. No one did. We just assumed they were something the Ochrans collected, perhaps as art objects."

Pennington was impressed, but not overwhelmed. "So why did they build cages down here?"

"What cages?" Pennington led him away from the body, with some difficulty, and showed him what she'd found. He shook his head. "I don't pretend to understand this. Perhaps they sacrificed one of the local animals as part of a memorial service. A companion for the afterlife, or food for the wandering spirits, or a propitiation of the gods and the price of passage to the Great Beyond. There are lots of possibilities and we may never figure which one is right."

McNabb knelt and began running his hand along the tops of the cages within reach, as though to reassure himself that they were real. Pennington glanced upward casually, then less than casually, and began shifting very slowly, letting her shoulder lights illuminate what she'd discovered.

"McNabb, you'd better look at this." Both sets of eyes followed the lights as Pennington illuminated each of the carved reliefs that decorated the walls surrounding them. At first they were unable to see the whole pattern, but eventually they recognized that there was a logical progression. It didn't matter where you started in the sequence, because like Ouroboros, it swallowed its own tail, creating a never ending cycle.

Pennington arbitrarily picked the simplest as the starting point. A stylized, almost stick figure Ochran stood with its limbs extended and a dark circle in the center of its upper chest, which Pennington assumed was meant to represent the heart shell. The adjacent panel was the same except that there was now a group of six small spherical symbols located in the lower torso arranged in a pyramid, one on two on three. The spheres were similarly arranged but noticeably larger in the following panel. In the next, the Ochran was in the same pose but with its head and limbs separated from the torso. The six spheres were now arranged in two pyramids, one on two, flanking the dismembered Ochran.

The Ochran was absent from the next few panels. The six small spheres were shown alone in the first, restored to a single pyramid, then dwindled to five, then four, the sequence ending with a panel in which only a single figure remained. It grew progressively larger in the next three panels, developing limbs and a head and terminating with the first panel she had examined, the single Ochran.

"It's a depiction of their biological life cycle," said McNabb, uncharacteristically subdued.

"This is a nursery," said Pennington. "This is where they came to bear their children." Her thoughts were racing.

McNabb lowered his eyes and shook his head. "Possibly, but we shouldn't leap to conclusions. And if that's the case, what are the cages for?" He scratched his head. "Maybe they fed some lower animal to their young until they were old enough to fend for themselves. It might have been a religious rite, an extension of primitive tribal customs. Possibly a young Ochran had to make its first kill before it was allowed to leave and become a member of the community."

But Pennington's thoughts were racing and she was far ahead of him. "No, that's not it. Remember the sandrunners, McNabb. That's the answer."

"What are you talking about?"

"Predation isn't nearly as big a factor on Ochre as it is elsewhere. Remember the sandrunners? They have no natural enemies and a single queen can produce thousands of offspring. A generation or two and they would have outstripped their food supply. So instead the young kill off the previous generation as well as a good number of their siblings before reaching adulthood. Plebeworms and several other species do much the same, and I think that pattern is reflected here. The Ochran children were savage, ravenous creatures. The mother, parent, whatever, died during childbirth, either naturally or because the children killed her. They devoured the body, leaving only the bones from which the shell, the heart casing or whatever it is, was set aside, to be honored or remembered. The children were then restrained and caged, to keep them from killing one another or maybe for the safety of the other adults. They were only let out once they had reached the next stage of their development, when they were more civilized. Or maybe only some of them were allowed to survive, to prevent the population from expanding too quickly. That's why they held them so deep in the mountain and made it difficult to travel between here and the surface. They weren't trying to keep intruders out; they were trying to keep their homicidal children in."

There was a long silence. "That's quite a theory to advance with so little evidence." But McNabb sounded thoughtful. "But that would mean that pregnancy was a death sentence."

"That's right. And maybe it was involuntary. At some point in their development, their bodies decided it was time to reproduce." Pennington started to laugh. She couldn't help herself.

McNabb stared at her as if she'd gone mad. "I don't see why you find this so funny. It's rather tragic if you think about it."

"McNabb, I think I know what happened to the Ochrans."

"You do? Marvelous!" McNabb had reverted to his normal sarcasm. "I had no idea that my guide was a trained xenoanthropologist."

She ignored his tone. "I think they got too civilized. They started enjoying life too much. They turned into your kind of people and it killed them."

"Did a rock fall on your head somewhere along the line, Pennington? You're not making any sense."

"Hear me out. It all falls together. The Ochrans die when they give birth, so they have to give up their own lives to keep the race going, right?" She didn't wait for an answer. "Well, what happens when they start figuring that their own individual lives are more important than having children? What if they found a way to inhibit the reproductive impulse so that they could live longer?"

"The birth rate goes down, obviously. But we're talking about a population of several million. What do you think happened? They all got together one day and decided that's it, we're going to have one big party and no more kids and that'll be the end of it?"

She shook her head. "No, not all at the same time. But once the idea took hold, it would spread, slowly maybe but surely. Fewer and fewer births until they dropped below the minimum threshold to keep the population up, then a slow slide toward extinction. If you had the choice between living a full life and having your kids tear you to pieces, which would you choose?"

"Well, obviously I'd choose to go on living, but I'm a human being. Assuming that you're right about their birth cycle, and I don't necessarily agree by the way, then they were accustomed to the situation. It was part of their natural order. Individuals who didn't conform would be viewed suspiciously, possibly ostracized or even persecuted."

"The early Christians were persecuted, until they became the majority. Times change."

"But that suggests that the Ochrans were an evolutionary dead end."

Pennington nodded. "Evolution doesn't work toward a goal. Sometimes short term advantages become disadvantageous in the long term. Which could be exactly what happened in this case, and that would explain why they're no longer with us."

"That sounds too simple. Intelligent beings are more tenacious than that," said McNabb, but he sounded uncertain.

Pennington laughed again, forced herself to stop. "I'm sorry. It's really not funny. But I just realized how much this discovery is going to annoy you."

"What are you talking about? This won't just show up Blumenthal for the superficial dilettante that he is. It will make my career."

"Yes, I suppose it will." Pennington felt almost lightheaded. "But you're going to have to modify one of your most cherished opinions. Don't you see, McNabb? This was an entire race of martyrs. Each and every one of them knew that the only way to have a child, to make sure the race continued, was to give up its own life. When the time came, however that was determined, each of them had to make the ultimate sacrifice for the good of the species. When they finally rebelled against their nature, they died out."

Pennington only had a second or two to enjoy the unhappy expression on McNabb's face, because that's when the earthquake started.

It wasn't a particularly violent quake, but it doesn't take much to generate catastrophic consequences when you're half a mile underground. They both froze instinctively, and felt great relief when the worst of the shaking stopped almost immediately. There was still a lot of noise, falling rocks, sliding sand, a steam vent somewhere screaming with outrage. But the ground stopped moving under their feet and the ceiling and walls hadn't collapsed on top of them, and they found themselves shaken but whole.

"I think perhaps it's time to go. There are bound to be aftershocks." Pennington was already on her way and McNabb, with one regretful glance at the dead Ochran, followed promptly in her wake.

Pennington knew that the most dangerous part of their escape route was the dizzying climb along the side wall of the immense cavern. The narrow ledge had been crumbling already; she would not have been surprised to find that it had broken away, in part or as a whole, leaving them stranded. But when they emerged from the tunnel and played their lights along its length, they could see no gaps, and a short time later they were both across, so badly shaken and trembling that they had to stop and rest despite their desire to escape what they now saw as a potential death trap.

As it happened, this brief respite was enough to alter their situation dramatically.

Pennington was the first to recover and stand, but McNabb followed suit without requiring encouragement. They entered the second stretch of tunnel but had only gone a few steps when the aftershock hit. It wasn't as strong as the initial jolt, but it capitalized on the wounds inflicted by the first. They both lost their footing and fell heavily, expecting to be buried in debris, but except for a pelting by small rocks and a sprinkle of sand, they remained uninjured when the worst of it was over.

Bruised but unbloodied, they exchanged nervous smiles as they regained their feet, but they were soon to discover that their situation had taken a turn for the worse.

They could no longer advance toward the surface, nor could they return the way they had just come. The rocky platform they had quitted moments before had broken off and fallen into the depths. More importantly, the way back to the surface appeared to be impassible and there were no alternate routes. Part of one wall had collapsed and fallen inward, silencing the intermittent steam vents they'd passed on the way in. There was theoretically still enough open space for them to skirt around the debris, but another obstacle rendered that impossible. The second, constant vent had narrowed, but even though its throat was more constricted than before, it was as hot and furious as ever. The result was a column of superheated steam that completely blocked their way, shrieking furiously as it lapped against the walls and, far above, an overhanging promontory.

"Now what?" shouted McNabb, whose eyes flickered with panic. He consulted his datapad again. "There's no other way out of here."

Pennington thought about it. "I guess we wait for a while and see if it stops." She settled down into a less than comfortable position with her back against the smooth wall, her face averted from the heat. "Unless you've got a better idea."

McNabb scrambled as far back from the vent as he could without risking a fall from the precipice to their rear. "What if it doesn't stop?" His voice shook.

"Then we'll probably die."

The vent refused to let up. The screaming changed pitch occasionally, and whenever that happened the two of them got to their feet, preparing to dash through to safety if the opportunity offered itself, but they were always disappointed. As nearly extinct volcanoes went, this one seemed pretty spry. The steam sputtered from time to time, the vent clearing its throat, but even then the plume was strong enough to burn their flesh. McNabb's biosuit would be no more protection than Pennington's more conventional garb.

After two hours had passed, Pennington decided that the mountain wasn't going to let them go voluntarily. She crawled forward, blinking as the hot air stung her face, until she was close enough to catch a glimpse of the interior of the vent during one of the flickers when the light wasn't quite as blinding. It was a flattened cone, wide at the top, narrow down below.

"What are you doing?" called McNabb, who had been watching uneasily.

"Evaluating our options." Her eyes were watering. Not only was it hot but it smelled bad, had worsened over the past hour or so. The fumes might be harmless, but they also might indicate that something toxic was bleeding into the vent. "We can't stay here," she shouted back. "If we stay, we die slowly even if there isn't another quake. So our only choice is to go forward."

McNabb folded his arms across his chest. "I'm open to suggestions, but I have an aversion to being parboiled."

Pennington retreated, wiping her face. "It looks to me like the vent gets very narrow about five meters down. If we can block it with something, even for a few seconds, we can get across."

McNabb nodded with limited enthusiasm. They made a quick search of their environment but were quickly frustrated. The narrow length of tunnel in which they were confined was almost featureless. The walls were either so solid that they could not break a manageable block of stone free or so grainy that pieces crumbled in their hands. There was nothing they could use to plug the hole. Small rocks and sand would simply fall through. They settled back down, discouraged, while Pennington thought furiously. There had to be a way out.

Several minutes passed before she raised her head, looked at her companion appraisingly. "Take off your biosuit," said Pennington at last, already undoing her own coveralls.

"Why?" McNabb had retreated to the edge of the chasm again, clearly despondent.

"Because I think we can jury rig our outfits into a kind of bundle. We fill them with sand, wait for the vent to stutter, and throw it in. With luck, we cut off most or all of the steam for just long enough to get past. We might still get singed but it's the best chance we've got."

It wasn't as easy in practice as it was in theory. By tying the sleeves together and using some of the tiny sensors inside McNabb's sophisticated biosuit as makeshift pins they were able to produce an ungainly container that was awkward to manipulate but which seemed to suit their needs. They filled the pockets with small rocks and the larger cavities with as much loose debris as they could manage. When they were done, it needed both of them to drag the ungainly parcel to the lip of the vent.

"We have to wait for it to slow down again before we push the bundle over." Pennington and McNabb were both sweating profusely now, their bodies streaked with grime, their fingers bleeding from their efforts to claw out the sand and crumbled stone.

Pennington's plan might have worked if McNabb had been content to wear ordinary desert clothing. But when the column of superheated air finally wavered and they pushed their awkward plug over the rim, the bio-sensors registered the sudden increase in heat and attempted to compensate. Micro-condensors switched on as seals locked and insulating pads inflated, both of which loosened the interface between McNabb's suit and Pennington's coveralls far enough to allow the upflowing steam to partially inflate it like a balloon. Most of the sand and stone spilled out instantly while the two suits, still locked together, shot up toward the ceiling and eventually fell on the opposite side, out of their reach. Pennington's clothing had been reduced to ash and McNabb's had melted into an unrecognizable blob that continued to sizzle and pop.

McNabb looked like he was going to cry. Pennington ignored him. She had a backup plan, but she didn't like it. "The principle was right. The materials were wrong."

"What the hell are you talking about? We don't have anything else to use." There was a sharp edge of panic in McNabb's voice.

"No, we still have one other option."

McNabb managed to look both skeptical and hopeful at the same time. "And what's that?"

"One of us can jump into the vent and block it long enough for the other to escape."

McNabb tried to laugh but it came out as a groan. "Anyone who did that would die within seconds in there. It's hot enough to boil the flesh right off our bones."

Pennington nodded, her face neutral. "That's right." She drew a deep breath. "So which one of us is willing to die for the other?"

"If you're expecting me to volunteer, you're out of your mind." McNabb took an involuntary step backward, but his eyes were alert, appraising. They were about the same size, McNabb a bit taller, Pennington slightly heavier.

Pennington held up a small stone so he could see it, closed her fist around it, and put both hands behind her back. "It's the only way, McNabb. Pick the stone and you jump. Pick the empty hand and I do the honors."

#

The authorities sent out an investigator and a rescue team by skimmer as soon as they received the emergency transmission from Teardrop. Although the survivor's message had indicated that it would be impossible to recover the body, they were constrained by law to at least make an initial attempt, and in any case the team leader would have to evaluate the situation to determine whether or not a more thorough investigation was necessary.

The flier put down in a cleared area not far from the cabin, and a figure emerged and started toward them even as they were climbing out. Proctor Brady gave brief instructions to her crew before starting up the path.

"So you've lost a client, Pennington," she said when the two figures met. "That won't look good when your license comes up for renewal."

Pennington shrugged. "It is what it is. Quakes are beyond my control, Angela. And the client refused to conform to standard safety practices. Kaffee?"

"Lead on."

They went inside the cabin where Pennington provided a condensed, edited description of the exploration of the cave system and what they'd found. Everything she said was true but she didn't say everything. Nor did she mention her theory about the Ochrans. The evidence was inconveniently out of reach and quite possibly permanently so. She had salvaged McNabb's datapad but it had been too badly damaged and the recordings were all lost. She did rather enjoy being the only person who knew the truth. On the other hand, if she had something to back up her theory, it would attract a horde of new researchers and she would be able to charge the limit for her services. But to do that, she would have to figure out a way to cap or bypass the vent and make new recordings of the birthing chamber.

Brady listened without comment until the end. "So once we knew that only one of us could get out of there, it was just a matter of deciding who was going to jump into the vent. I give McNabb full credit. He gave his life for me."

"And just how was that decision made?" Brady gave no hint that she was considering the possibility of foul play.

"Pure chance. I put a pebble in one fist and told McNabb to choose a hand. He chose the wrong one, luckily for me."

"Well," she sighed. She wasn't sure if she should believe Pennington's account, but it would be difficult to prove otherwise. "It's a shame, but at least he died well. No chance of recovering his body, you said?"

Pennington shook her head. "It'd only be bones by now, if they haven't been vaporized as well."

"Well, we'll have to take a look for form's sake, and there'll be more questions to answer back in Lachrymosia, but I'd say you were off the hook. This time." She stood up. "I'll get my team together and with luck we can be out of here before dark."

Pennington stood up too. "I'll take you up there as soon as you're ready, but there's not much to see."

Brady left and Pennington returned to her seat, finished the last of her kaffee, and idly rubbed her sore knuckles. She'd dislocated one of her fingers as well and even with a shot of Numball, it was giving her a lot of pain. With her good hand she reached into a pocket and brought forth a piece of smooth stone small enough to hold in her clenched fist.

She told herself that she would have jumped if McNabb had chosen the right hand, but he hadn't so she would never know. At the last moment, she might have discovered that her own instinct to survive was stronger than her intellectual admiration for self sacrifice. Certainly the issue had not been in doubt in McNabb's case. He had folded his arms and refused categorically to die for her, although ultimately he had done exactly that.

Pennington rubbed her aching knuckles. It had just required some persuasion on her part.

www.ingramcontent.com/pod-product-compliance
Lightning Source LLC
Chambersburg PA
CBHW072143170626
46813CB00004BA/1656